Diary of a Witchcraft Shop 2

Trevor Jones and Liz Williams

Diary of a Witchcraft Shop 2

Trevor Jones and Liz Williams

Ably assisted by the Voodoo Boys:
Jamie Alexzander and Jack Snell

Illustrations by Liz Williams

NewCon Press
England

First published in the UK June 2013 by NewCon Press
41 Wheatsheaf Road, Alconbury Weston, Cambs, PE28 4LF

NCP 053 (signed hardback)

NCP 054 (softback)

10 9 8 7 6 5 4 3 2 1

ISBN:

978-1-907069-45-1 (hardback)

978-1-907069-46-8 (softback)

Cover art and internal illustrations by Liz Williams

Cover layout and design by Andy Bigwood

Minor editorial meddling by Ian Whates

Book layout by Storm Constantine

Introduction

Since the first Diary of a Witchcraft Shop was released, we still run a witchcraft shop, and we still don't have enough demons. When Trevor and I wrote the first volume of Diary, we hoped that people would find our adventures amusing, and indeed, they seem to have done so. Those adventures actually took place over a couple of years, condensed into a single 'diary' year, and this diary is the same; hence we seem to take more trips than other people, and have more arguments. The events in this second volume take place roughly from 2008 – 2012, but following the same month-by-month basis.

Animals have come and gone, and so have people: the most significant folk to join us on the good ship Witchcraft Ltd in recent years have been Jamie Alexzander and Jack Snell, known to many as the 'Voodoo boys' and now running their own business as occult consultants in addition to retailers. Without their hard work, determination and thankfully sharp tongues, life would have been a great deal more difficult than it has been over the past three years, and I thank them.

We hope you enjoy this edition of Diary as much as the last one, and we hope you'll come and visit us in Glastonbury and see all this for yourselves. Those who have done so have rapidly realised that we've had to tone things down rather than exaggerate them, and believe me, there is quite a lot we've had to leave out...

April

Voodoo

We had a staff training evening tonight for the new voodoo products, hosted by their creators, the voodoo boys. We are going to have to have the occult equivalent of a sharps bin, as some of the powders will, according to Jamie, hex you the minute they are touched with bare hands.

Staff member: So what happens if you handle them with gloves?

Jamie: Then you'll have cursed gloves.

And people ask me where I get my ideas from.

*

In the evening, T and I were invited to the Faery Ball, which is a regular event here. Lots of people dressed up, quite spectacularly. On hearing that I was going to attend this, *my own mother*, on the phone, remarked – "What are you – the Evil Fairy?"

Spring out there

Last week was busy, and this week will be, too. We have a house guest at the moment, so she and I headed out onto the Levels this morning and took separate walks (purely because she wanted to go to a particular place, and you're not allowed to walk dogs there because of otters). So I took them down a very silent track past an old farmhouse and into the woods, which is all part of the reserve. There are celandines in the hedgerows and out in the orchard, and the hawthorn is starting to come out into leaf. It's been rather a chilly official equinox, but spring has now sprung.

We saw the 'supermoon' on Saturday night – enormous, and hanging over the Tor.

*

Doing Latin Homework. Again. It is Forty YEARS since I had to decline 3f. Sigh...

Cambridge

We have been in Cambridge, at the now two-yearly college alumni dinner. Good to see Magdalene again – I am reminded that it has been a part of my life now for exactly half my life – and great to see Kari and Phil and their incomparable cats. We spent Sunday strolling around the Backs, which are glorious at this time of year – full of daffodils, narcissi and hyacinths, with the ducks nesting between them. And then caught up with the Cambridge Blue and the Kingston – the Blue, in particular, was my local for a time over 20 years ago.

Pity about the Boat Race, but we've become resigned to that.

We came back via Buckinghamshire and then Avebury, where we stopped to see a huge, hazy crimson sun going down behind the stones. Returned to find that the dog sitters have done an admirable job and the dogs have created no havoc whatsoever. At least, none that I have found.

*

This morning, Glastonbury is basking in the spring sunshine and adjusting to the clocks going forward. Customers are strolling about, the people at the market cross are arguing, but gently, and a gentleman whom I shall call A is having a long and involved conversation outside the local cafe with Andy McNab about a SAS operation. It might, somewhat worryingly, be better if Andy McNab was actually there, but A obviously feels that he is: if you shut your eyes, it is a very convincing dialogue.

Zap!

I am just enchanted – literally – to learn that one of the diocesan exorcists has a Gryffindor 'wand' with which to change the TV channel.

*

This from the Glastonbury Radio newsroom – although I can't help feeling it is depressing news...

Breaking news for your show... KFC have today confirmed that a site near to B & Q in Glastonbury is "under offer" for a new drive-thru KFC! Meanwhile under the Travelodge, two new units will be opening soon, one a Subway, the other a Domino's Pizza!

Conferences

This weekend has been conference-tastic, with the symposium on Friday that we have been organising for the last six months or so.

The symposium came about because of the increasing numbers of academics (sociologists, anthropologists, historians) who have been coming to Glastonbury, and sending students on theology courses. It is a diverse community, which, despite our difficulties, possesses a remarkable degree of coherence and tolerance. The place is increasingly becoming an object of study, and the symposium was set up to explore the various ways in which we, as a community, might support future research. Speakers were Ronald Hutton, Marion Bowman (OU), Miguel Farias (Oxford) and Sarah Goldingay (Exeter), Denise Cush (BSU) and John Wadsworth, who is a local writer. Mainly academics attended but there were also some local writers, and the symposium generally seems to have gone very well: it was extremely diverse, with witches and priests (all of whom went down the pub later). Currently, Janet and Gavin are running a workshop up at the Grail Centre now, while Trevor and I try to catch our breath.

*

Academia Alert – skip if bored now! Got my Open University Archaeology course assignment back from my tutor yesterday. He made no comments on the essay itself – which is fair enough because it was a month late. Gave me 89% for it though...

Tintagel

We've been down to Cornwall for twenty-four hours – wild and windy, with thundering seas off the north Cornish coast. In Merlin's Cave the whole cave floor was covered with a shivering mass of foam, like something out of Dr Who, and when the wind changed direction it flew out of the cave mouth in gobbets. We stayed at the wonderfully eccentric Castle Hotel, which is about as close to the sea as you can get without falling in. There's a great photo of the Castle against a blue sky with the owner's new Bentley in front of it, entitled International Headquarters of World Media Inc or some such: it's like Thunderbirds. We wondered if they have secret vaults under the cliffs with experimental technology. Up the stairs were testimonials by guests ("Visiting your hotel changed my entire destiny").

On every pillow was a poem on magic, written by the proprietor.

But it's lovely. It's like being in an Arthurian film set of the 190s. The views are incredible, the food and service are good, the staff are charming and helpful and it's very reasonably priced. I suggested to Trevor that, since I had a druidic robe with me for various reasons, I did my Vivian Leigh impersonation and ran shrieking up and down the corridors, but this idea was, strangely, vetoed.

In the morning, we headed up onto Bodmin Moor and the Hurlers standing stone circle, getting very wet in the process, and ended up for lunch in Jamaica Inn. You can't resist lunch at a place that flies the Jolly Roger.

But Daddy…

I am due to start work on a short term teaching contract at Bath Spa university today. Just walked into the kitchen to find T saying to a dog, "Mummy doesn't love us any more, and that's why she's leaving. But *daddy* loves you."

Fully expect to return to find the dog on the phone to his psychiatrist.

Lunatics and Lockdown

We were about to make some lunch when a staff member rang to say that another business colleague had been into the shop, and told her that someone was threatening to come to our house with a sledgehammer.

I rang the contact, who said that this is a woman who has been around town for the last couple of weeks. I met her a few days ago, and she is clearly very fragile and unstable. It turns out that she had a reading from our new lodger at a psychic fair a short time ago, and halfway through the reading informed him that they were destined to be soulmates. Lodger immediately called a halt and told her to see a therapist, but Bunny Boiler, as I will call her, has clearly not taken this advice. She has been writing him sixteen page letters, and left incessant phone messages.

She spoke to another staff member, who said that she was manic, vaguely recognising that something was wrong, and panicking as a result. When she spoke to me she was fairly calm, but clearly in trouble.

Anyway, Bunny Boiler came into another shop this morning, told them that she was carrying a knife, which she has been brandishing around, and was planning to come to the house, at which point they called the police.

Many conversations with the law later, she turned up at the front door at our home, with a knife. Trevor told her to put it down, leave, and never come back, otherwise he'd kill her, and he intimidated her so much that she actually left.

We are in lockdown, and instructed to call the police if she returns. Hopefully, they will pick her up in town this evening as I suspect she has gone back there to seek Lodger.

Next day, I have spoken to Lodger, who has had a call from Bunny Boiler and told her not to come to the house, because she won't be able to get hold of him there. Apparently she has a history of depression and attempted overdoses, during one of which her first child died (we're not sure how). Her parents are now seeking custody of the remaining kids.

Trevor had to go and do something this morning and forgot he was due to give a talk at the local psychic fair, so I did it instead. Afterwards, I had a chat to the audience and mentioned we'd had recent difficulties with a customer: "Oh yes," a woman said. "Is that P's stalker?"

I have told Lodger that we are renewing the shotgun license.

*

How am I supposed to get the Latin done when I have a fifty pound puppy on my keyboard? Lily wants attention...

Eastercon – Good Friday

We came up yesterday and had lunch in a nice pub outside Worcester, then drove straight into the NEC, parked without incident, unloaded, and were set up in the Dealer's Room by 4. Spent the rest of the afternoon in the countryside around Stratford, which is glorious at this time of year, then went into Henley-in-Arden for dinner. We found a nice gastro pub which is selling my cousin's beer, so yay for Purity, then returned to my cousin, who lives nearby.

Dr Who/Torchwood writer, Paul Cornell, and I did an Easter/Spring Equinox ritual at the convention: when I asked the ritual question, "What does spring mean to you?" Paul replied "Regeneration!"

Warwickshire and Gloucestershire were glorious. We then went up to London on the following Wednesday for the Clarke Awards – these went well and we were introduced to the delightful Little Georgia restaurant. I like Hackney and we also went to the Dove, which is one of my favourite London pubs. We wandered around Whitechapel market buying unusual vegetables, but had to interrupt this with a very tedious visit to the bank – an enormous queue and only a handful of bank tellers. Eventually a man with no chin emerged from the back regions and on being accosted, said that he 'was not allowed to engage with customers,' whereupon a large and angry man decked with gold chains and tattoos remarked, "Of course 'e 'aint! 'E's in the back eating fucking biscuits!"

May

We got into work this morning to find that someone has left a fake stuffed crow on the doorstep of another shop, so we have been fielding, and repudiating, suggestions that it might be our staff – happily, the entire street is on CCTV so we quickly realised that the person who did it will be on record.

Jamie and Jack were indignant and say that had it been them, it would have been 'a real crow with blood and everything'. It's the implied lack of style that's offended everyone so much.

However, relations are still civil and we suspect Bunny Boiler. Lodger has run her out of town, apparently, although I am sceptical about the staying power of this.

*

Later Jamie and I were doing the window, when a dishevelled person came in and announced their shock at finding out that I am real. Replied that the whole moving and talking thing was a bit of a giveaway.

*

STUDY! Despite the universe throwing things at us. Positive things maybe, but there to distract if I let them. We won't be fooled again...

Birds, Beasts and Victorian Engineers

This week seems to have brought wildlife out all over the place – goldfinches, herons, cuckoos and Canada geese out on the bird reserve. Both geese and swans are followed by skeins of toddling fluffy babies. Here in the orchard we have a tree full of owls: I haven't seen them but I can hear them. During the heavy rain last week, we met several displaced water rats and there was a big hare in the stubble of the corn field a couple of days ago.

At present, someone has put three ponies in our back field: they were initially offhand and then realised that we came bearing carrots, at which point they have become very very friendly. They have a spindly foal, with a ridiculous (but natural) New Romantic pompom hairdo.

Otherwise, it has been a busy week – we went up to Bristol for the Leonardo Da Vinci drawings exhibition on Monday (including a beautiful sketch of oak leaves) and spent an hour or so in Bristol museum. Staff changes currently mean that we get two days off, which is good for the mental health.

Yesterday, we hosted a steampunk handfasting in the orchard – the sight of seventy Victorian engineers and their wives among the apple blossom is one that I shall treasure for some time to come.

*

We had to stay in town today to meet P, the local blacksmith, who has been making cat and cauldron shaped brackets for, natch, the Cat and Cauldron.

The brackets are great.

P met me in the pub fifteen minutes after he'd started.

Me: That was quick! [pause] Oh.

It turns out that the building is so old that it is not entirely clear to anyone what is holding the front of it up, and the chances of the whole lot falling off and leaving P standing in a window frame like Buster Keaton, are high.

We will have to speak to the landlord and see if there's any way another bracket bit can be put on to fix the bracket to. P's last comment on the matter was "And I'd have gotten away with it, too, if it hadn't been for those pesky kids."

Spring. Sprung?

Spring has visibly begun to move on the Levels: pussy willow is on its way out, the hazel catkins have been out for nearly a couple of weeks, our garden is a mass of snowdrops, and the crocus and daffodils are starting to put in an appearance. It feels softer and lighter, although there's still a raw edge to the wind and since Trevor has experienced snow on his birthday before now (which is in June), no one is holding their breath. I have vases full of mimosa, hyacinths, narcissi and iris at home.

We have been on a couple of long walks – one to the bird reserve, which is filling up with wild ducks and swans, and one to Berrow flats and the beach. I thought we were in for a storm last night, but I woke to a very fiery sunrise this morning.

We made it to Wells market yesterday – a very busy farmers' market – and I notice that people are branching out into things like cupcakes and macaroons, as well as a couple of stalls selling very good vegetarian and Indian food. Jamie and I were supposed to be going up to Bristol today and the Chinese warehouse, but this has been postponed and I've been spending my unexpectedly free morning dealing with housework, paperwork, and manuscripts. I will be finishing off this quarter's short stories this afternoon – as well as a heavy teaching load in the last week, one of the stories just hasn't gelled... until it suddenly did. That happens.

Bloomsbury and Spare

Up to London on Monday for a meeting with the writing mentoring organisation whom I work for. We had lunch at The Booking Office at St Pancras which, somewhat confusingly, is a brasserie. Once our meeting was finished, I nipped into the British Library to see the new SF exhibition, which is a lot of fun – they have some very good exhibitions in that downstairs section. I then walked down to Bloomsbury and visited Treadwells' new, larger shop – great to see everyone – and had an early dinner in Museum Street before catching the bus home.

Treadwells and Christina furnished me with Phil Baker's new bio of Austin Osman Spare, a fascinating character on whom the Cuming Museum in Southwark ran a very good exhibition last year. I gather there's a new documentary coming out soon, as the London literati cotton on to what ceremonial magicians have known for years – that someone of remarkable artistic calibre was living in obscurity for decades in Borough. Unlike his contemporary Augustus John, Spare could not bring himself to paint socialites and the wealthy – an early brush with his own celebrity in his teenage years seems to have put him off – and he painted people in pubs and the local market women instead, and lived with a horde of cats made homeless by the Blitz. Alan Moore, in his excellent introduction to Baker's equally excellent bio, compares him to that 'other south London angel-headed nut-job, William Blake.'

Training Ground

I like students, and as druids, witches etc, we are here to answer questions, but full-scale interviews for people's academic theses need to be set up in advance. I work all today, then have to go home and do housework, and am then teaching for the rest of the week. I have just had to explain to a nice young German boy that (a) Glastonbury may appear to be full of hippies but we still need to do VAT returns, stock checks etc, (b) we work for a living full time and can't just drop everything to go off for a couple of hours and (c) yes, Glastonbury has been affected by the recession because it *is part of the real world.*

The vast majority of our customers know this. Glastonbury is often a sanctuary to them and they treat it as such (which we encourage – we're holders of the space, allowing visitors to do what they need to do here, but we don't always have that luxury). But they're usually mature enough not to see it as a sort of bubble apart from the rest of the world. We're not, in the main, the cynical exploiters of legend: the magical and esoteric side of the place is also very real, and if I could float it away through the mists where the tax man couldn't find it, I would! But I can't.

German boy has now been appraised of these basic facts. Sigh.

The Commute

I have been teaching. This entails rising at 6.30 and driving to Bath. Half an hour of the journey, which takes about an hour and a quarter, is within Bath itself: not a town built for the motor vehicle. It is in fact less than thirty miles away – we are in a Bath postcode here in Glastonbury. But old winding country roads, agricultural vehicles and in the city, modern traffic, means that it's a slow trip.

It is, however, beautiful. The journey takes me over the hills, which are filled with beech woods, bluebells and wild garlic, and through the kind of villages that get used for locations in English cosy murder mysteries. Once we get to Bath itself, I drive up past the Royal Crescent, which in early morning sunshine is something else. The university department is on a hill, and looks out across the city to the countryside beyond (Bath is not big). It's in an old part of the city, and there are some stunning gardens filled with roses, odd secret passageways, sudden flights of steps and arches in Bath's weathered golden/grey stone. On one side is an enormous manicured park, and on the other, in front of yet another crescent, is a long sweep of railed grass in which I discovered a small, placid flock of sheep. This in the middle of the city.

And on the way home is the Farrington Gurney farm shop, currently advertising Gert Posh Teas.

*

Getting back into the multicultural waters of EFL has been entertaining, as always. My class is composed of Japanese and Arabic students, and there's a bit of a gender split as well (all the Arabs, bar one, are male).

There are some issues you just can't get into.

Me: So, do people go to restaurants a lot in your country?
Arabic student: Um. The men do.

And this morning another teacher started to deal with conversational English for ordinary situations, like a restaurant.

Teacher: In a restaurant, you *order*. In your home, you *ask*.

Student: Actually, no, I order at home.

T: So, what, you look at a menu at the dinner table at home? You have a personal chef?

S [slightly surprised]: Yes.

T: Ah.

S: It is the same in all Arab states, in Saudi. [then becomes aware that his fellow Arabs are looking at him very strangely.]

Second Arabic student: Er, we don't have a chef. Unless you're super rich.

One of my colleagues has run into additional geographical problems and has had to abandon Things of Geographic Note in Japan (e.g. Mt Fuji) and concentrate on such Tokyo landmarks as H&M, the Gap, and TopShop.

*

Note to nameless person: five days/forty hours a week, starting at 10 am, is not 'far too much work' for someone in their early 50s. It's actually a normal working week for most people and lightweight for some. Ah, Glastonbury, home of the over-entitled. (Not one of my employees, thankfully).

*

Today I have to cram twenty-one days of Latin homework into about six hours. As a card-carrying Gemini, there are times when I hate my procrastination.

*

I am proud to say that even the part-time staff were visited by the sarcasm fairy in their cradles.

Loud kid runs into the shop. His obnoxious dad grabs him

by his hoody and drags him out.

Dad: Don't go in there, they'll turn you into a toad!"

L: We don't have to – the job's obviously already been done by his father...

*

Trevor overheard someone questioning what the hell his wife might learn from our workshop programme – advertised in the window.

Trevor: Maybe acquiring some fucking manners?

[wife comes in, grinning broadly; husband remains outside, face thunderous].

*

Group of male teenagers come in, spot naked god pictures, start macho sniggering.

F: [in bright Scottish tones] Now, lads – no need to be jealous!

Teenagers: shuffle feet. Leave.

Law and Order

I have spent half my evening at the Dion Fortune reading group and the other half at a town council security meeting, to address issues with the police about anti-social behaviour in Glastonbury. There are three main factions: youths/adults on weekend nights, which make the town centre effectively a no-go area; the junkies who hang out by the church, and the traveller group who has taken over one of the car parks. They all have a set of things in common: drugs (mainly dope and heroin) or alcohol, extreme aggression and a complete unwillingness to engage with the mainstream, even such as it is in this very alternative town.

Our main beat copper couldn't make it tonight, due to being kicked in the throat during an altercation at lunchtime yesterday, but his boss was there and they are starting to prosecute and fine people, which seems to be having an effect. They can now fine parents who supply their kids with alcohol – most of the troublemakers a couple of weeks ago were too young to drink legally and were carrying booze given to them by their parents, e.g. bottles of vodka. The junkies are a constant problem and used to be policed by the rest of the street community (we know one of them, who says they basically used to beat people up and dump them outside town if they got out of order, which was a lot more effective). Rehab here just doesn't seem to work. I suspect the police are being circumspect about the travellers, due to race relations legislation (although if this particular group of people come from an ancient and dignified non-British culture, I'll eat my hat. My late partner did come from that background and was not positive about it, nor about people who constantly sentimentalised it because they were feeling guilty about being middle class and had never actually met anyone from it).

And someone who was not me mentioned vigilantes, which is what is going to happen if the police strategy does not prove effective over the summer. Fingers crossed that their operation works.

*

Jon passed on this quote of the day – 'Adults are just children who owe money'... Hmmm...

*

I had a series of academic meetings today to sort out the summer school and talk to the teacher with whom I'll be running the Japanese programme. J is a very nice guy and we had a good meeting. He has taught at the university before and at the end of the meeting leaned across to my boss, G, and said, simply, "By the way, I'm *so sorry*."

"I don't want to talk about it," she said, very tight lipped, then added, after a moment's reflection, "We only needed ONE GOAL! One goal – how hard could it be?"

She's from Tyneside. Alan Shearer is her hero. Enough said.

*

Some weeks ago, Glastonbury planned a May Day celebration. All was progressing normally, when one of the (few) rabid Christians around here wrote to the local county paper with a claim that the committee had been taken over by Satanists and were planning an orgy in the woods. Disgruntled that it had not been told, the committee set up a Facebook page for people who would like to be invited to an (entirely mythical) orgy. I gather from members of the local congregation that the writer's behaviour is, let us say, challenging.

The person who wrote to the paper is frequently in various newspaper columns, commenting on her ancestor, Druid William Price, who was quite a cool dude to whom we owe the legality of cremation in this country, but who was also into nudism, vegetarianism and wearing a red boiler suit covered in magical sigils: in the 1890s, this was considered a trifle odd.

I mentioned this to the local paper, and the woman replied with a rather peculiar letter, suggesting that I fear the power of Dr Price. I have, naturally, responded, never being one to let a good grudge die quietly.

She was, quite soon after, sectioned.

*

Scene: the shop in Benedict Street.

All the customers are female.

Customer 1 [striding in, decked with a lot of pentacles and, I fear, a tie-dyed velvet dress]: [dramatic gesture] YOUR SHRINE MUST COME DOWN! THERE IS A BAD ENERGY TO IT! I... AM A PAGAN HIGH PRIESTESS!!!

Customer 2 [before Jamie can respond]: You're a fucking idiot!

C1: Whaaa- but I am a HIGH PRIESTESS!

C2: You're an idiot! If you haven't got anything constructive to say, piss off!

C1: But –

C2: OUT!!!! [is echoed by Greek chorus of other customers]
Jamie: Thanks very much. Have some incense.

Trevor Jones, B.A.

Trevor's graduation ceremony took place in Torquay yesterday (no Fawlty Towers jokes, please!) and it all went very smoothly, from arriving in Torquay to discover that £7.00 + of car parking had been commuted to £1.00 for the entire weekend, as a result of a special offer, to the pub at the end of the road that did quick lunches, to the ceremony itself. Trevor has now been duly beaned, suffered a free glass of champagne, and then we hightailed it to Dartmouth, the car ferry, and subsequently the Cherub pub, which dates from 1380 and is small, low-ceilinged, friendly and bears a remarkably good selection of single malts.

The Tour is Here

Got into town at the crack of dawn this morning to park and found that the town has been transformed overnight for the cycle Tour of Britain – tons of infrastructure has pitched up. The bands have started and the actual race is due to arrive in about half an hour: they are belting up from Devon. There are events into the night, including a fireworks display in the Abbey.

Note to the local drug dealer: ranting because your access to the road is restricted isn't intelligent, but doing it in front of the Drugs Testing Tent *really* isn't.

June

Exmoor

It being Mr Jones' birthday week, we ran away to Exmoor: walked in larch woods and on bilberry moors, had lunch in a hotel in Dulverton where the dogs copped three lots of dog biscuits from admiring bar staff, and then drove to the old bridge at Tarr Steps. Here, things went somewhat awry: Trevor had to swerve to avoid a teenage idiot driving far too fast in the opposite direction, hit a rock and ripped the front tyre out. Luckily, this happened at the entrance to the car park and the warden let us use the landline to call the AA. While perfectly capable of changing a tyre, the bolt that secured the spare wheel to the frame had rusted up and could not be moved: the AA man had to use a hacksaw to remove it. While we waited, we took it in turns to go down to the bridge, but it did not, in fact, take long and we were in time for dinner.

*

Desperately trying to get some study done and the puppy has learnt to bark at everything – and she has just pulled the wireless router off the shelf...

Jubilation

So, Jubilee weekend is upon us. Glastonbury is celebrating with music at the Abbey, a street party this evening, and a torchlit Tor on Monday – I rather like the whole beacon fires resonance about this. Since we're not big on street parties and it is, needless to say, raining, we have come back to roast lamb and a bottle of wine, but tomorrow we are heading to the other side of the country to conduct a handfasting and visit friends in Cambridge.

However, the countryside is looking glorious and there is some fairly restrained bunting all over the place. The council have hung the flag on the front of one of our shops upside down, and someone further up the High St has replaced their Union Jack altogether with the Lion of Judah.

Barges

We drove across the country in the rain yesterday to Essex, a part of the country which I don't know at all well, but this bit of it was extremely pretty. We had to conduct a handfasting, which was supposed to be in a meadow but which ended up in a boathouse instead, due to the weather. This all went smoothly except that in the pub beforehand, having changed my clothes, I lost the car key and found that I had inexplicably hidden it in my shoe.

It was a very English wedding, with cake, homemade cheese straws, elderflower cordial and tea. And rain. There were bee orchids on the lawn and the roses were out. After this, we reached Cambridge in the early evening and went out mob-handed to the Shanghai Family restaurant, one of our favourites.

With regard to the Jubilee, we've just caught up with the pictures of the Thames flotilla, which looked great: lots and lots of little boats, chugging madly up the Thames. I liked the bell barge, which rung out the bells as they went and were answered by the churches. I also like the Spirit of Chartwell, with its decorations of Thames waterfowl: kingfishers, herons, cormorants. Having seen the alternatives to monarchy, I would rather stick with what we've got and I am in favour of tradition: Glastonbury beat the bounds on Saturday, and there have been a lot of low-key, informal community events, fuelled by tea.

Tonight, we have beacon lighting, Her Maj *"will trigger the lighting of the final beacon by placing a huge crystal into a specially designed pod."* Followed by a fly-by on behalf of the British Space Corps and as my friend Kari suggested, a loop-the-loop by the Duke of Edinburgh with his jetpack.

Beacon

Spent Monday lunchtime in a fabulous pub called the Queen's Head at Newton in Cambridgeshire. This serves soup (colour coded: we had 'dark reddish brown'), which was excellent, toast and dripping, and sandwiches. And that's it, food-wise. The bar has not been decorated since 1945. In a case on the wall is a stuffed goose: Belinda, who used to patrol the car park and hiss at people.

Then we drove back to Glastonbury, celebrated Trevor's birthday further by going out to dinner, then went into town to see the beacon lighting. When we got there, even though it was still broad daylight, the beacon was blazing away: apparently someone lit it two hours early, thus pre-empting the Queen and indeed, the rest of the country. However, the ceremony went ahead and the whole Tor was strung with torches like a processional way. With the full moon rising alongside, it looked like an enormous liner sailing across the Levels. The crowds were so thick that we did not climb the Tor, but went and watched from the windows of the gallery, just down the road. Apparently everyone on top of the hill – the clergy, the Mayor, random occultists and the local Druids – all led the singing of *Jerusalem*.

Duck!

People possibly think I make stuff up for this diary. I never do. If anything, I downplay it.

That being out of the way, some explanation is needed: things occasionally get broken in the shop. When that happens, we can either throw the item out (a waste), or find something else to do with it, and the 'something else' usually involves giving it to the local animal sanctuary. They repair the broken stock, sell it in a jumble sale, and thus benefit rescued animals.

Today, Sanctuary Woman comes to pick up some stuff.

Me: How are you guys getting on?

SW: Okay! Except we had a baby pheasant at the weekend, who died. And a duck who is at the vet.

Me: Oh no – what's up with the duck?

SW: Its willy won't go back in.

Me: !!!

SW: [impervious to shock] no, his willy has got stuck and we can't get it back in.

Me: [finding power of speech] I had no idea that could happen to ducks. I didn't even know they had them. I thought they had a kind of slot.

SW: It happens a lot and the last time it happened, it dried up and fell off.

Me: [unable to stop myself] Good thing that doesn't happen to men, eh?

SW: [slightly startled] Um, I suppose so!

Trevor now tells me that his conversation with SW, who is elderly and very sincere, involved her attempts to replace the rogue avian dick – "we found some grease, but then suddenly there was stuff all over my hand." Nooooooooooooooooooo!

If It's June, There Must Be Druids....

It is five in the morning. I am sitting on a bus outside Stonehenge. The driver of the bus is engaging with the Stonehenge gate guard who is refusing to let anyone in until nine a.m. even though we have booked. He is about to meet a hundred and fifty really irritated druids.

*

We spent yesterday at the Druidic Summer Assembly, preparing for a ritual at the top of the Tor in the afternoon (sunny until we finished, but graced with lots of dancing fritillaries), then at the evening's entertainment. After an hour's sleep, I got up at 3.15 and went back into town to catch the bus to Stonehenge (see above). We did get in, although it's infuriating to have been doing this on the same weekend for fifteen years and to be suddenly denied access because someone hasn't communicated something to someone else.

At this time of the morning, the henge was beautiful – there was a ground mist throughout Somerset, with the tree tops floating above it. Venus was very bright above the ruins of the Abbey when I arrived back in Glastonbury. We saw hares in the fields and owls going home in the halflight. By the time we got into the stones, the larks were all up and singing.

The ceremony went well although it is not the Solstice yet. OBOD always has its big public solstice rites the week before, so that individual groups can do their own on the actual date. But it is a conveyor belt at this time of year – there was another group waiting to come in once we'd finished.

I went to sleep in the orchard this afternoon with the dog tethered to my wrist: this was not a success as Lily got bored and attacked my pillow, then ran round and round until she snarled me up in her leash, and then dug a huge hole and covered me in earth. She has had the same length of day that I've had. We've had house guests but everything was quiet in this house at 3.30 am except for pup. Pup was up!

*

Yesterday, in his address, Philip C-G mentioned that there was something to celebrate: namely, it's now umpty-hundred years since we got rid of the Romans. Cue a cry from the back of the hall in an Italian accent: "And now – we're back!"

We have had forty Italian druids in town this weekend. They did a lovely dance presentation this morning, looking very Vestal (okay, wrong pantheon – but we're not worried about that these days).

*

From the Never argue with a Rottweiler dept – I am probably going to have not one but TWO dogs with me at work today – Tara is thirteen now, but every now and then she just feels like a chauffeur-driven ride to see her estates in

Glastonbury. Lily comes with me most days anyway, and has her own fan-club in town. Tara is sitting hopefully by the car-keys.

*

As you do, I am studying the structure of Roman barrack buildings on Hadrian's Wall... and sometimes being Pagan helps. Just got to the final block of research for this essay – turns out it is on the subject of Ephesian Artemis – a subject which, 'cos I is pagan, I might already know just enough about, to avoid a week's reading – YIPPEE!!!!!

Newcon Press and 'Glass of Shadow' Launch

We came up to London on Friday for the launch of my short story collection – Anna is very kindly putting us up. Headed out to Queen's Park and a rather good gastro pub called the Alice House, which serves cocktails in teapots (we stuck to the wheat beer). Yesterday, we caught the bus into town, heading past a lot of Trevor's childhood haunts in Maida Vale and around Marble Arch, arriving early in Holborn. We wandered around for a bit, looked at some remarkably overpriced jewellery in Hatton Garden and stumbled over a magic shop – the other sort of magic – which has apparently been there for fifty four years. I had a long conversation with them, mainly about my dad and their upcoming conjuring convention.

Then we headed to the Cittie of Yorke, encountering Ians Whates and Watson en route. What a spectacular pub it is, with a high beamed ceiling and vast barrels. The room where we held the book launch is like a gentleman's club – panelled, with leather sofas. Later, the long main bar became filled with a collection of lawyers, Guardsmen (with spurs) and subsequently the Met, lots of them, and all rather grim, who hauled out a number of disreputable blokes who had been in a fight down the road, run into the pub and hidden in the toilets (when I mentioned this to a woman at the launch, she said "How old are they – six?")

Ian thinks that more than eighty people came. It was great to catch up with everyone, and to see Tanith Lee, John Kaiine, Anne Sudworth and co, and to meet Storm Constantine, who did the layout on my short story collection. She was one of the first people to publish me, over a decade ago, in *Visionary Tongue*, which was in hard copy then. Also great to see Peter Lavery, my now-retired editor at Macmillan.

We left the pub about 7 pm and headed into Bloomsbury, splitting up in order to eat. Trevor and I ended up in Kimchee, which is a big Korean place. I had bibimbap, which I like but which means that the word gets stuck in my head ("Bibimbap! Bibimbap"). I'm sure this is very childish but some words just *do* that. Then we headed back to Kilburn and are now winding gently into Sunday: a trip to the local Asian supermarkets was called for before we head out.

Camping

Our temporary resident campers returned last night from a festival but stayed in the house, due to rain.

A: I know you're not going to believe this, but... you go into their bathroom, and there's a toilet which has a seat.

B: No!

A: And when you look into it... you can only see water, and both sides of the bowl. And it's clean!

B: Next thing, you'll be telling me you can flush it!

*

Clever Lilypup knew something was wrong in the kitchen and said so in no uncertain terms – growling and yapping at it. A dried-out pan about to catch fire on the hob – eeek! Clever Lily saves the day – but the house stinks...

Daisy Chains

My students pleaded to have their class outside today, which is left up to the teacher's discretion, so we did. They read out loud and made daisy chains, just as I read out loud and made daisy chains thirty years ago on a similar school lawn.

Otherwise, it's been a day of dog walking – Lily put up a partridge yesterday and a small egret today, and has not yet learned that flying things cannot be caught, at least not easily. Yesterday we found a dead swan on the Levels and have taken the long pinions for various magical bits and pieces. Everything is coming out in a rush – alder, ash, which always looks as though it has exploded, and the grass is thick with dandelions, ladies' smock and celandine.

We're eating leeks and purple sprouting broccoli from the garden, and our co-gardener has been planting a ton of stuff – garlic, beans, peas and Jerusalem artichokes amongst them.

*

Jamie has mentioned the Welsh mother and daughter who were in today:

"What's that thing for?"

"It's for divination," the daughter chirps up. "Nanny's got that."

To which the mother replied "No, luv. Nanny's got Dementia."

*

We have had a highly entertaining evening out with former Radio Caroline and Radio 1 DJ Paul Burnett, who is doing some stuff for Glastonbury Radio. A number of former Radio 1 DJs are doing work for the radio station at the moment and it is very odd meeting people whom one listened to in one's teens.

However, Paul is a delightful man and extremely funny, and told me a quite appalling story about being forced to drink aviation fuel by Vietnam vets years ago at a gig in Germany. A cocktail known as an afterburner, apparently, for reasons which should be obvious.

*

We have a new supplier who deals in skins, skulls and bones. She has given us a spare fox skin. Her house is full of bits, in various stages of treatment (so is our house, to a much lesser extent). Her husband apologised as we came in. "Sorry about the mess," he said. "My wife lives here."

"I never really," she said, "got into the whole housework thing."

*

You have a business. You give the business a page on Facebook (for announcements etc). You send those of your employees who have an FB page an invite. They don't respond. Then they complain (not to you) that they should have been officially told about the Facebook page.

*

On the news that Russians were being encouraged to drink Malt Whisky to stave off Swine Flu –

So THAT is who is behind the pandemic panic nonsense – the DISTILLERIES!!!

Avebury

We had to do a handfasting at Avebury today, on the Solstice itself. We made it up to Avebury in good time, and the weather held out. We found a parking spot without difficulty although there was a queue when we left, waiting to come into the car park. We also had a nice lunch in the Red Lion, which was quite quiet. So the only drawback was the absence of the happy couple: this arrangement dates back to April and we'd laid on staff. Trevor had an email on Thursday to ask if we were still on for it and I replied with my mobile number, and asked for the handfastee's number. I didn't get a reply, and they didn't show up today, though we sat in the pub for three hours over lunch and coffee, nor did they call.

The police were there in force, mainly for traffic although

there was a plain clothes detective questioning the more obvious travellers. As he was wearing a suit and carrying a clipboard, he was the most conspicuous man for about five miles. Someone told me that one of the squad cars was the armed response unit, but I don't know whether this is true – it seems like a lot of overkill for a fairly sedate pagan gathering. I understand there's a zero tolerance policy at the henge this summer, though.

The Science Bit

Despite a long train ride and being late, I got to Imperial College late in the morning for a very interesting one day conference for SF writers and physicists, organised by the university. Writers included Geoff Ryman, Paul McAuley, Stephen Baxter, Al Reynolds, Pat Cadigan, Ken McLeod and various other folk. We were given a series of lectures on cosmology, the solar system, a day in the life of an astronomer and other subjects.

There seems to be a trend this year of putting scientists together with writers (obviously, several writers *are* scientists), starting at the London SF film festival and going forward into the autumn when I've been asked to do an event with my writing team person at Manchester. As a writer who has a sort-of science background (philosophy of science and AI), but who is lamentably aware of their ignorance in many fields, I find all this very interesting.

Also you have to like a place which has big instructions in all the lifts telling you not to get in them alongside canisters of liquid nitrogen. Cue image of frozen authors toppling forward and shattering on Imperial's floor.

*

...amazed how full the shop gets every time a new rain shower opens up. Funny that...

The Religion Bit

I have been doing a great many things over the last few days and it has not quite stopped today, as a friend asked me if I would be willing to talk to a Christian retreat, staying at the Glastonbury Abbey's extremely beautiful guest house. They asked a great many questions, all thoughtful and thought provoking, and were extremely pleasant. They are a liberal group, interested in exploring different spiritualities.

Archaeology

We went to the Crickley Hill archaeological dig's annual reunion dinner yesterday evening, catching up with people I haven't seen for twenty years.

We had a talk on the dig by Phil Dixon, who was the site director. The dig ended fifteen years ago, but with two million finds, it's still being written up. Archaeology takes a long time! Odd to think that all the little fragments of pot that I spent carefully categorising in the finds hut on wet afternoons are still being catalogued at Nottingham University.

The dig started in 1969, when archaeology was a very different animal. Phil fondly remembers a large chunk of rock dropping off the side of a cutting onto the unsuspecting head of a digger. This was in the days before health and safety kicked in, so the victim was not wearing a hard hat, but a straw boater, in, Phil said, an attempt to lend some class to the proceedings. The rock laid him out but didn't actually kill him and he appears to have taken it in his stride (this was also in the days before we were so litigious).

The thing that most intrigued me was a stray comment about one of the younger guys who was there last night. His grandfather (I think) was a dry stone waller (Crickley is at the edge of the limestone Cotswold scarp) and remembered being told by his great great uncle about the 'people who lived in the little thatched cottages on top of Crickley, in the days before the Romans came.' This story was told to the granddad around the 1900s, way before archaeologists had any idea that the hill fort had housed roundhouse settlements, so it seems to be a folk memory. It gave me a very odd feeling to look at the young man across the bar, two miles from Crickley, and think that his ancestors might have lived in the area for over 2000 years. The occupation of the hill fort itself goes back by about 4500 years.

*

On most archaeological sites, it's the people as much as the things that you remember. Some finds obviously stick in my mind – a 17th century scabbard, a Roman belt buckle in the shape of a seahorse – but as Phil remarked, sometimes it's hard to remember that we were actually there to do a job.

Most sites have their resident eccentrics, archaeology being a profession that attracts ripe old characters and allows amateur input, and Crickley was no exception. (If you think I know some odd people now, you must understand that this has been going on for most of my life.) Ours included Britain's top test pilot, who on days offsite occasionally used to do test runs to Anglesey. Peacefully peering into a cutting, people would become suddenly aware that a Tornado bomber was hurtling towards them out of a clear sky and more nervous diggers occasionally threw themselves flat just as he pulled out of a dive. I don't think this was actually sanctioned by the RAF, but it was entertaining.

There was also Arwel, who was involved in inspecting nuclear plants and was a member of the Territorial Army. He was continually inventing things and I have a memory of something called Arwel's Patent Leg, but we now have no idea what this was (I asked him last night and he couldn't remember either).

Also present last night was JP, Crickley's own resident provo, although as far as anyone could determine, he had never actually been to Ireland (or indeed, far from Ross on Wye). JP was not infrequently malevolent and used to lurch up and down the site cursing in what I gather is quite a rare Forest of Dean dialect. He used to tell us a series of bizarre anecdotes, involving a cast of dramatis personae that included the SAS (who are based not far away in Hereford), his half-sister Yasmin, and various denizens of Ross.

Eventually, the assistant site director and I wrote down the titles of these stories on the back of an envelope – I have no recollection of doing this, but the envelope was produced last night and it's my writing. We think we can dimly remember the story about the E-type Jag and the sten gun, but the precise contents of story number 22, 'The Bishop of Hereford's Answerphone' have eluded us.

Art

On the landing this morning, a profound installation making evocative use of organic and inorganic materials, plus a wide sense of dynamic spatial awareness. I have utilised found objects, deemed to be 'garbage' by the mundane world, in an attempt to demonstrate the inherent futility of existence and the interpretation of canine agency within it.

I have decided not to take heed of my critics' uncomprehending words ("That was my sponge! And what the hell happened to this loo roll??"), or their pathetic failure to understand my genius. Clearly post modernism is beyond them, but I am an Artist, and must endure.

Lily

*

If anyone is wondering what the upshot of last month's voodoo customer episode was, Jamie has spoken to the customer on the phone and apparently he is very pleased, as someone tried to shoot him last week and the gun did not go off; proof to him that he is under a protection wider than that of human agency.

Let's hope it lasts.

July

Cackle

It must be a real slow news day – Liz may be on BBC Radio Somerset tomorrow morning for a telephone interview, giving advice to prospective candidates for a new job as the witch at Wookey Hole – and I quote, 'to cackle in the caves'. The money they are offering…

We subsequently had to give advice to an American TV reporter, sent to audition for the part.

A Viking They Did Go…

A writer friend, Patricia Kennealy Morrison, has been staying with us for the last few days and we have had a delightful time – I picked her up in Oxford's beautiful Christ Church on Saturday and we drove down through Avebury, where we had lunch. Patricia is writing a book on the Vikings, which partly takes place in this area, and so we have been to Barrow Mump, to Wedmore and Edington, and to Wells. I have learned a great deal about my own county – I am familiar with the Arthurian cycle, and with later aspects of the county's history, but know next to nothing about the Saxon/Viking period. We also went to Lyme Regis, where a seagull snatched a sandwich out of my hand in an immediate surgical strike, and home via the Cerne Abbas giant.

Queen of the Night

We are going to a handfasting this evening, focused around Hekate, of whom the couple are both followers, and our friend A ordered two red mullet from her fishmmonger and had them shipped over. Red mullet is a sacred offering to Hekate, along with garlic. Something has, however, gone horribly awry in translation and instead of two red mullet, Jamie has a box of twenty four mackerel. A thinks that this will enrage the Queen of the Damned and cause her to flood Glastonbury. I have suggested a barbeque. Either that or we'll all be clutching one at the wedding, like a little fishy bouquet.

More Art
Dear Artist Friends,

It has gladdened my little dog heart to see how much support there has been for my artistic endeavours. Already I feel less alone and am planning a truly major work, although I might have to wait until I am bigger and can break into the large white box where they keep the food.

And yet I can rely on no assistance here. For some reason, the Philistine who lives here laughed like a drain when she read your moving Facebook posts, which I found very unfeeling and just goes to show how little she understands a true aesthetic sensibility. But with your help I think I can find the strength to go on.

Lilypup, Artist

Tibet Week
This is Glastonbury Tibet week and for the last five days crimson robed monks have been wandering about all over town. They have constructed a quite magnificent sand mandala over the last few days and are now deconstructing it.

I spoke to one of the monks and they like Glastonbury, partly because people don't stare and point at them (I am typical in having walked past two of the monks on Wednesday and not realising until some minutes later, simply because we get so many visitors of so many different faiths). But they like it and want to come back. They're from a South Indian monastery, being in exile. I think they are supporters of the Panchen Lama.

Turkey Shoot
Our lodger has a male friend. The friend plays practical jokes.

This week's include: Deep Heat in P's shampoo, and the re-arrangement in road signs to make P late for work.

So last night, as the friend was collecting his girlfriend from the airport, to return to a newly cleaned flat, P gave him two unexpected house guests. Two large bronze-winged turkeys.

I gather they got into the larder.

Oh For...
The Sun newspaper just rang up my staff to ask if the pigeon on the Algerian Goalpost was sent to curse the English World Cup team.

It's So Spiritual...
In the Magick Box. The sun is shining, the sky is blue. Soft music is playing in the background. The scent of incense drifts down the High St from a dozen doorways.

Customer: Oh WOW, it's so amazing in here! I live in Essex and this is the first time *I've* been here, this is such an amazing town, it's so spiritual and everyone's so lovely...

Me: it is rather unique.

[*Trevor: on Yahoo Messenger:* Pop! I just decked Resident Druggie. Fortunately off camera]

Customer: everywhere feels so calm!

Me: [Oscar-worthy performance] Yes, it's very peaceful.

[*Me, on Messenger:* What exactly did you do??]

[*Trevor on Messenger:* smacked him straight in the back of the head 'cos he was winding up L. He fell out of the shop door and landed in the road.]

Customer leaves on a cloud of well-being. Which cannot be said for all of us.

The Dog Ate My Homework

There are some students who, it must be said, are not really into the whole studying ethic. There are some students whose embassy is overseeing their stay, as they clearly recognise that there is an issue. There are some students who will come up with a quite remarkable range of excuses to escape this gross intrusion into their leisure time.

F: I am looking at you, as I do not entirely believe that your brother coincidentally suffered a car crash within minutes of you passing your test for a foundation course, and is now in a coma which requires you to bail on the rest of the programme and fly back home. Forgive me for being a shade cynical.

PS: no, we don't really think you have swine flu, either. That was just your teacher being sarcastic.

X: if you say to your teacher (not me), "I can't come to class this afternoon. I have to – [pause for thought]", and your teacher says "What is it this time? Going to the bank?" it is not tactful to reply, "No, I've already used that one."

Y: if you tell someone that you will not be in school because you are busy, and they say, "Why?" replying "Because I have lots of things to do," doesn't really cut it.

The Witch of Wookey

Our American TV presenter was pipped at the post by a local estate agent, who says, worryingly, that she regards cavern-dwelling witchcraft as one step up from being an estate agent.

Still, she was wearing one of our hats, so go that customer! Trevor said to her, "You should get the job for the green nails alone..."

Also, kudos to the woman who brought her own raven.

Carla Calamity just came in to say thanks for the wand. One reason she got the job as the Witch of Wookey was that she had a selenite rod from us – and when she waved it at the press, it SHATTERED in three parts!

A Sense of Déjà Vu

I am concerned that one of my staff members might be going round the bend, again (you'll remember the Queen of the Fairies). A demon, she says, attacked her when she was vacuuming the shop. She blames Jamie and Jack, and says that she should not have to worry about other employees, even though we are beginning to be fairly sure that she has destroyed computer records so that they will get into trouble, and loses no opportunity to complain about them.

I've been keeping an eye on this particular staff member for some time, ever since she informed me that I 'was not worthy' to receive her expertise and wisdom on the Tarot.

Well, Do You Want Me...?

Met the landlord of our local pub in our other local pub this evening, which was oddly mind-bending. Conversation turned to waiting staff, and X reminisced about a particular waitress who used to serve in a pub in Bristol near the law courts, and who was once caught coming out of the kitchen with her thumb on a steak, thus nailing it to the plate as she carried it. When remonstrated with, she replied, "Well, do you want me to drop it on the floor like the last one?"

Déjà Vu 2

Having been left with little choice following a serious complaint by a customer, I have fired our probably-going-mad employee. At home, her boyfriend is having to 'pull spirits out of her back'.

She has previously told me that she was cursed in her home country, and that she and her brother are alien abductees. As long as staff turn up on time and sell stuff to people, I don't mind, but there are limits, which rudeness to customers, intimidation of other staff members and attempts at manipulation significantly cross.

I have had a certain amount of feedback from Jamie, so I collared our lodger a couple of nights ago and interrogated him.

He doesn't know the boys all that well, but does know Employee, and said pretty much word for word what I'd had from the boys. It dovetails a bit too much with my own experiences and rather than waiting until an explosion occurred, I decided to pull the plug.

I don't like doing this sort of thing. But I will do it if I have to. Bloody Glastonbury! Why can't they just nick pound coins out of the till and smoke illegally in the lavatory like every other sackee?

*

Woke this morning with a sense of relief in being rid of ExEmployee – now rechristened Exployee. So that the rumour mill didn't get in first, I have emailed a few people and it looks increasingly likely that the plastic crow left in our competitor's doorway a few weeks ago was down to her (we later confirmed, via CCTV, that it was).

The Evil Eye

When I was a small child, my father very irresponsibly told me that the family had the evil eye, so we did not have to take action when people shafted us, as they would soon die.

Irresponsible, but reassuring.

Trevor, on the other hand, is a Gemini and just lets things happen around him.

The story so far: a friend had a brief fling with a remarkably unpleasant woman who used to be in the South African police (enough said). It didn't last. I had a row with SA Policewoman over a business matter, and threw her out of the shop. She is now terrified of me and, indeed, there is a part of me that is not displeased that I can apparently intimidate members of the SA police force. A low part, but hey.

One of our former art suppliers is an older lady who has a history of lying to us, and eventually went off to sell stock to a competitor. Apparently she has had a fire at the factory which makes her sculpture moulds, is no longer producing work, and has had to let out half of her house to a lodger.

Guess who the lodger turns out to be?

South African Policewoman has moved in with our ex-supplier, an event which threw everyone, as previously they lived on the other side of the country to one another (the supplier is in Cornwall). Trevor hoped they would be very miserable together.

This evening, in the middle of a book launch, someone rang me to say that South African Policewoman has done a flit, taking all our ex supplier's furniture, including the light fittings and, enterprisingly, the fireplace, and stiffing her for £600 in rent.

I shall leave it to you to draw your own conclusions, except to say that dinner tonight consisted of some pasta, and a side order of chilled vengeance.

Sicilians

I've started teaching a two week contract with an early commute to Bristol. My colleagues are all lovely and have the world-weariness that is typical of the career language teacher.

The students are Sicilian, teenagers, and in some cases male. I don't think I need to unpack this for you. Yesterday, one of them turned to his teacher and said "I think you 'ate me." To which she replied, "You're not wrong."

It's going to be a long nine days.

*

There has, to date, been reasonably little fall-out from my sacking of Exployee. Trevor went into one of the local crystal shops and was informed by its proprietor that Ex came in some while ago, to berate him for selling obsidian mirrors too cheaply, and said that he was damaging 'her' business, of which she was in charge.

Crystal Shop Proprietor told her to fuck off, which I feel is a wholly appropriate response. Meanwhile, more has come to light from other staff members, which makes me feel deeply relieved that I sacked her. It amounts to harassment, if not intimidation.

What follows is very unprofessional, but I am sick of giving these assholes so much leeway. I have now had to fire two employees for going mad in a very similar way, and it is unfair on the rest of the team to have them take out their massive ego trips on other people. In Ex's case, I think she thought that I'd believe her – so calm, grounded and conscientious – over two young men whom we don't know very well. Jack and Jamie were targeted by Ex to the extent that they kept an incident log, very sensibly, and did things such as keep their own day sheets, in case she tried to alter records, which she did. However, like most manipulative people, she had failed to realise that she'd already established her own track record in this sort of thing long before the Voodoo Boys came on board and her behaviour towards them only consolidated my worsening opinion of her.

Anyway, we found a card in the rack which gave various options: 'our sympathies on your sacking/demonic possession /alien attack/psychotic episode'.

Inside, there are other 'condolence' options. I gather that Jamie ticked the top option, and two of the ones inside ('job loss' and 'psychotic episode.'). There are a number of other options ('strange interlude') which might also be apposite. He is going to post it tonight.

A friend of his, in the shop at the time, said "Liz didn't *tell* you to send that, did she?" to which Jamie replied, "Liz simply handed me the bullet. *I* shall fire the gun."

Wifelet

The rumour mill launches into its summer action with the magnificent fiction that I am having an affair with Lord Bath. I would love this to be true, but alas, have never met this particular aristo, although Trevor knows him slightly. Maybe Trevor is having an affair with him instead?

Public Post from Trevor (in the window)

To the extremely childish and rather pathetic person who spread some dubious and entirely ineffectual 'magical' shit over the step of the Witchcraft Shop – grow up fast – you will be receiving a visit from the local constabulary. You are NAILED – sucker...

Baphomet
For the Brits, my friend Julian will be on the 4th Plinth in Week 8, dressed up as Baphomet, like you do, and raising the profile of the Museum of Witchcraft in Boscastle.

*

Was this morning faced with having to explain carefully to a non-resident what 'the 4th plinth' is, and why one of our foremost Chaos Magicians should want to expend perfectly good drinking time on it being gawped at by tourists.

Mud Wrestling
All I can say in the town's defence is that we have no television sets in Somerset and therefore must make our own fun. This brought to you by the local estate agents (the magnificent Mr Bending. Regular readers may recall the house that was advertised with its own flight of rooks):

On the release of the video covering the First Goddess Mud Wrestling Championships (Only in Glastonbury dept) –

I am indebted to Brian Visiondanz (now sadly no longer with us) for this erudite peek into the higher reaches of Glastonbury culture.

Feedback
Trevor got an email from a close friend last night, who mentioned that she had been to her Druid grove meeting a day or so ago and one of the others had mentioned going into one of our shops at the Assembly. She and her friends were apparently treated to a rant by the shop assistant about how Druids were all 'weak' and 'spiritual vegetarians.' They left without buying anything.

Needless to say, I checked who was on the rota that day, and it was Exployee. She was a member of my order, but wasn't allowed to move up a grade (probably due to signs of being bonkers, which I suspect her tutor saw), so left. I'm going to write to the druid and offer her and her friends a discount.

Exployee is about to find out what a spiritual carnivore is like, i.e. me.

*

After the latest sacking, someone asked me whether we were just unlucky or whether this was somehow endemic to Glastonbury.

Well.....

Hopefuls often give us CV's. Last one was a girl so stunning I forgot to actually read it! Given recent events, Liz did...

She has spent the last 8 years writing poetry in Lithuanian, which admittedly is her native language.

Under 'achievements' was listed a 2 day training course by a hobby-craft shop, ability as a poet, and as a third point the words "I am!"

Despite a vague resemblance to Descartes' ontological argument for the existence of God, a consultation with my co-director has revealed that *being* is a necessary but not a sufficient condition for employment with us.

The candidate also possesses a 'rare maturity' for her age and 'a profound intelligence that does not conform to logical standards'. Her writing has apparently moved people to tears, but whether these are sobs of ennui or simply those of hysterical laughter remains to be seen.

In counteraction to my raising these points, my co-director replied in each instance that "she was very pretty." Whilst sympathetic, I have been forced to invoke the iron bar of those self-same logical standards and state that we will not be employing this person anytime soon, as in, before Hell freezes over.

August

High Summer

It is rather lovely at the moment – shorn wheat fields on the university road studded with oak trees, the mown hay fields covered in flocks of terns and rooks, hanging baskets tumbling with flowers in all the little villages. Here, the hawthorn berries are turning red and the rowan trees this year on either side of our gate have produced enormous bunches of scarlet berries, too.

*

S, a friend of our new lodger E, is staying with E to attend the Goddess Conference. She has Carla the husky with her and today left Carla in the flat with the windows open. With the result that as I was standing at the back door, there was a sudden terrible scrabbling and a husky shot down the roof and fell twelve feet into a bush.

Luckily, she is all right, but we have brought her into town, where she is undertaking occasional dominance competitions with Cass and being admired by customers.

*

We have spent the day down on Exmoor with Lily – a long walk across the heathery moors to Dunkery Beacon, and then we drove down to the coast and Porlock Weir via Horner Woods. Exmoor is very atmospheric in this rainy light. Lots of bilberries!

Oxbridge

Trevor and I departed for Cambridge on Thursday, heading up through West Wycombe for lunch at a pub that has an Old Skool White Lady as its resident ghost (unglimpsed) and a visit to

Dashwood's caves: always entertaining. Thus lunched, we drove through heavy rain to Cambridge, arriving barely unscathed due a somewhat alarming brake and skid on the M25: we stopped about a foot from the bumper of the car in front, and the Merc behind stopped a foot behind us. Glad I'd just had the car MOT'd and a new tyre in place.

The purpose of the Cambridge leg of the visit was the Cambridge Beer Festival: this was very civilised if a little wet. Trevor stuck to stouts and porters and I stuck to anything whose name I liked – a very good lavender honey beer stands out, but they were all pretty good. There were a lot of local breweries whose products we just don't see in the West Country.

White Queen

We went to an Alice-themed birthday party last night and our friend A, along with two of her friends, dressed up. They visited the supermarket before they came to the party, where A, who was dressed as the White Queen, endured some abuse from local youths until one of their friends said, "Oi! Leave her alone! It's her big day! Never mind, love – you just enjoy your wedding."

Since A was in a vast confection of white, accompanied by a man in a fake zebra coat and top hat and another man dressed as a rabbit, we have no idea what kind of wedding they thought this was going to be.

Gypsy Curse

It was extremely wet this morning and quite cold, but has now cleared into blazing sunshine. I took the back roads home through Godney – lovely pale fields of wheat stubble and all the hedgerows were heavy with ripening berries. I was not, however, whelmed by the old gypsy lady driving a Vardo, for whom I had to back into a ditch, receiving a mouthful of abuse as I did so, and no thanks when I had done so. She could have been the model for Granny Weatherwax, but was even less polite (I put a hex on her – sometimes the witch is the one driving the Peugeot).

She is not the only person driving a wagon around the landscape: there are lots of vardos, some really rather pretty, trundling about like snails, parked on roundabouts and verges. At least Granny W's horse looked reasonably well-cared for, which is by no means standard.

*

An armchair has been dumped in the horse trough. Yesterday the special brew drongos were using it. I'd so like to pass a current through it.

*

The perils of crystal balls, one of which has just caused a small fire in someone's front window.

Oh Deary Deary me...

As Nuala put it so well – I'll repeat what she said –

"Thought for the day: keep your balls off the TV; nuff said..."

*

We went out with a friend, M, last night, who when at theological college in Dublin many years ago, organised a charity event. He booked eight bands but needed nine, and so, when walking along the street, he saw a slightly bohemian-looking bloke whom he vaguely recognised as a musician, he stopped him.

"How's it going?" M said.

"Fine!" said the bloke. "How about you?"

M explained about the gig. "Would you be up for it?" he asked.

"Sure!"

"Only I'm afraid we'll need a demo tape..."

"Not a problem," said the bloke. "I'll send one to you."

"And," said M, embarrassed, "I'm terribly sorry but I'm afraid I've forgotten your name."

"It's Bono," said the bloke. "See you there!"

M was so mortified that he told U2's lead singer that it

wouldn't be necessary, but was equally certain that they would have turned up had he pursued it.

*

Had a real magical experience listening to Holst's Jupiter in a field, gazing at planet and moons through giant telescopes. Thanks Charles!

This evening we went to a very good open air concert just south of Glastonbury, conducted by the BBC's Charles Hazlewood (in his back field, basically) – an orchestra doing Holst's Planet Suite. In between planets, he had a subsidiary group as a response orchestra, improvising 'replies' to each movement. I gather this group includes members of Goldfrapp and Portishead, so they're used to innovative material, and what they did was interesting.

As they played, Jupiter rose like a lamp in the south, along with a clear half moon – the concert team had provided a bank of telescopes through which you could look and I watched a tiny moon sail in front of Jupiter's stripy disc.

Bournemouth

Jamie and I drove down to Bournemouth yesterday for the first annual conference of the Bournemouth Pagan Society. I did a (debunking) talk on magic and quantum theory. Kim Huggens did a very interesting talk on Mithraism – they invented the hot cross bun, apparently, and some of the statues in early Mithraeums had movable mouths, suggesting the presence of a bloke behind them with a flamethrower.

My old friend Julian Vayne did a talk on the history of magic and I fear that fatigue caught up with me. I went to sleep on a nearby sofa, waking in time for a shout of 'Hail Satan!' from the entire room. So I shouted 'Hail Satan!' too and then went back to sleep, waking much later with the terrible fear that I had in fact dreamed this, and the BPS had been subjected to the sight of one of its speakers suddenly waking up at the back of the room, uttering an invocation to the Devil and then passing out again. However, it turned out to have been real, happily.

*

Glorious late summer sun over the bird reserve – Egret, Buzzards, Reed Warblers, several species of duck and a mute swan looking after her cygnets by swearing at Lily!

Mearekatz.com

I am startled to discover that all the time we have been sitting at home, posting on social media about tomatoes and the dog, we have actually been running a wife swapping club. Who knew? This is the latest instalment of the Glastonbury Rumour Mill. Trevor has decided to call it 'MeareKatz', like LOLcats, after the name of our village. Simples! Please send your car keys via our website.

We will be charging for this essential rural service. £500 per annum will get you a joining pack, plus a pair of free furry handcuffs, a bottle of lube, and a false identity.

I suppose I should be taking this more seriously. But I just can't. The great advantage of the rumour mill is that you can have a really exciting virtual life, while in reality, you are pottering about making cups of tea and watching the news.

*

Trevor's response to the WIFE-SWAPPING club rumours – Cass is under the weather. She came to us looking like she was either in season or just going out – and sure enough, she has been grumpy for the last few days... She has also trodden on something awkwardly and has a sore paw. She is going to be let to rest that today, while we go in to town and arrange this weekend's Swingers roundabout...

*

So, this rumour about wife swapping came out last night in

conversation with a writer who has just moved to Glastonbury. A couple of years ago, he gave a tarot reading to Exployee, shortly before moving back to the US. Earlier in the year, Ex started writing to him – ten page emails in which she dictated whom Writer was allowed to speak to when he returned to Glastonbury. This was before Ex got fired, but apparently Writer was under no circumstances to speak to us, as we were 'evil.'

Writer thought he'd make up his own mind, thanks very much. He is staying with a mutual friend. A month or so ago, Writer went out to dinner with us and that was apparently the cue for hysterical phone calls from Ex to the effect that Writer had 'betrayed' her. Note – they'd met once before Writer moved back here.

Anyway, Writer says that Ex loathed us long before I fired her, because, as far as we can make out, she thinks I was her mother in a past life. She's been spreading a whole load of allegations around town, rather as the pathetic Queen of the Fairies did, but like QOF, is increasingly running out of anyone who will listen to her.

Writer said that he ran into Ex in Wells last week and did his best to avoid her: he said that Ex's face was contorted with anger and Writer did not want to engage, but did say 'hello' when spotted. When he quickly walked off, Ex marched after him, mimicking his accent nastily all the way down the street. I am going to speak to the police – there's nothing they can do, but at least it is a paper trail. I gather Ex has been reported to the cops before, for writing anonymous letters.

*

I have spent the afternoon in one of the shops, covering for a sick staff member, and have had conversations with at least two people and one email regarding the Exployee. The general consensus? Mad. Although there was a suggestion from someone I barely know that she is a 'paid troll from the dark side'. I thought that was just the internet?

Meanwhile a solicitor's letter is being composed. Those of us who have been involved are continuing to act with dignity and restraint – i.e. not posting a fake obituary in the Free Ad paper, or putting up WANTED: MY MISSING SANITY posters on lamp-posts. It is good to see that after four years in this town I retain the vestiges of an ethical system, though admittedly only just.

Non-Government Health Warning

Thoroughly enjoyed my curry and beer last night, but feel I should perhaps have warned the clan that I had beans for lunch...

*

I have managed to have another row with someone, this time in the street. We'll call her Rat Girl, since she has a long, twitching pink nose, little beady eyes and sharp teeth. And a history of pilfering, which goes with her general totem-territory. She used to work alongside Trevor, years ago now, but did not last long and she usually avoids us. I threw her out of the shop for being the source of many of the rumours that beset the town, and shouted at her on the pavement in front of about a hundred horrified customers of the local café. Like most innate bullies, when confronted, Rat Girl burst into tears and fled, and is now presenting herself as a hard-done-by-waif, which nobody can bring themselves to believe.

The REAL Swingers

Exhausted after a session with twenty swingers in Wells... One National guitar (replica) and nineteen other sundry instruments for a blues jam (get your minds out of the gutter). I really should have taken the 12 string. I've been promising for three years now!

Teri, We've Told You Before...

In other news, Jamie has been plagued by a stranger than usual customer this morning; on first opening. A woman came in – petite, nicely dressed etc – and informed him that she was being haunted. By Teri Hatcher. Who, as far as I know, isn't dead. I did think of writing to Ms Hatcher, who happens to be the friend of a friend of a friend (six degrees sort of thing) along the lines of 'Teri! We've had words about this before! Now *stop haunting people*!' I have suggested to Jamie that it would be entertaining in a sick sort of way if 'celebrity stalking' meant just that ('I found that Tom Cruise going through the bins again this morning').

I See Stupid People
In response to someone's appalling behaviour (in this case, Rat Girl) as a 'High Priestess', you write a blog post outlining the behaviour, and some examples.

You send the person a link, with a terse (actually, an extremely rude) message instructing her to read it.

The person is – result! – upset, and tells a mutual acquaintance that 'the post was clearly about them.'

Of course it was about you, you halfwit! That's why I sent you the link in the first place!

Message to a Florist in the Area
A colleague told me she had to intervene last summer when a florist put big labels outside the shop advertising the pretty trailing blue plant that you buy for your hanging baskets.

It's 'lobelia.'

Not 'Labia.'

Helping the Police with Their Enquiries
Rat Girl, despite having a criminal record, apparently called the cops because I shouted at her. Conversation went like this:

Policewoman: I'm here to see –
Jamie: Liz Williams.
Policewoman: Yes, how did you –
Jamie: Let me guess. Rat Girl. Accusation of assault?
Policewoman: Ah. Has she done this before?
Jamie: A number of times.

Policewoman: I see. Well, she's a very silly woman, then. Is Dr Williams available?

[Short pause while I am summoned]

Me: Yes, I shouted at her and threw her out of the shop. Convictions of theft, etc etc. don't want her on my premises, etc etc...

Policewoman: She hasn't actually made a complaint, just expressed concern at the language used and – [the strange small cat Phineas appears] Oh! *Look* at his little face!

And that was that.

September

Autumn

There's a very autumnal feel to Somerset at the moment – when I woke this morning, the fields were wreathed in a light mist and there was a pair of deer in the opposite field, the buck grazing along the hedge. It smells like autumn, too. We had an early start and I went over to Wells market: picked up some lamb and a purple cauliflower.

We had to go down to Minehead yesterday and the countryside looks fantastic – deep red or brown ploughed fields and the hay all in bales. We're supposed to have our back field cut soon – had to move the pony into the orchard, which freaks out the dogs (MUM! There's a horse! There's a HORSE!). This is in payment for some ram's horns – one of those weird local trades, i.e. someone gives you some horns and is paid in hay.

Excitement of the following day was that Trevor appeared in the shop shortly after I'd got back from the market and told me that the dog had wandered off. Ran all over town, enlisting the help of the local gypsy women (my High Street Irregulars) and then discovered that he'd locked her in the bathroom.

Exhibitions

Tired but happy. A full weekend on the shop, and Liz was taking a group of aspiring creative writers through the process of getting published. In between all that, a massively successful book launch with new author Vikki Bramshaw, and today a major new art exhibition in Glastonbury by our very own Anne Sudworth. A hectic, exhausting, but intensely pleasurable weekend. For once, Mr Grumpy stayed at home today...

*

Almost like a mini-convention – we had the launch of Anne Sudworth's wonderful exhibition at the gallery on Sunday. About a hundred people came throughout the afternoon, including a lot of folk from the British SF scene whom we don't usually see in Glastonbury. In the evening, the G&P was wall-to-wall Goth, but they seemed to cope! Yesterday we met up with a friend from Magdalene in the evening and had a great evening out near Bristol. So it has been a very social few days. I'm currently in the gallery for most of the week, and writing Worldsoul in between visitors.

*

I told the latest set of handfastees when we met last Friday, that I hoped September mists would close in and the sun would come out during our brief time at the stones. Druid weather magic did its best – a wonderful shroud at Stonehenge and a great ceremony, and the sun shone through at the end. I am proud of that.

Glastonbury Conference for the Fantastic in Literature

Well, we had it, under the aegis of the Write Fantastic! And it was great fun. Speakers included Freda Warrington, Kari Maund on the historical origins of Arthur, Paul Weston on John Cowper Powys, Yuri Leitch on Katharine Maltwood, and myself.

*

We had a great offer yesterday – an eighteen year old girl wanted to sell her grandmother's 12th Century Book of Shadows. An unbroken tradition dating back to Norman times – WOW! When Jamie questioned her veracity, curiously, she backed off and left in a hurry. We can't think why.

A Day for Doreen

Dogs guarding the fort. A Day for Doreen Valiente. Off to

London for some esoteric stimulus. Roman History course book to read on the train.

*

Trevor and I went up to London by train, arriving in the nick of time at the hall in Red Lion Square. The day itself took the form of a series of short talks by people who remembered senior witch Doreen Valiente, and was organised by John Belham Payne, who has inherited much of her magical tools. I have to say that John and his cohorts did an excellent job and were extremely pleasant and helpful when there was a slight mix up over our tickets.

Guests included Ronald Hutton, Janet Farrar and Gavin Bone, Marion Green, Maxine Sanders, Lois Bourne, Ralph Harvey and Fred Lamont, among others, and everyone had something interesting to say.

The concrete results of the day for us are that I will be doing some archiving work over the next few weeks for Marion and that Ralph will hopefully be coming down to Glastonbury in November to do a book signing (he is, he said, playing Capt Mainwaring in local theatre. Told him that I hoped he got to say '*Stupid* boy,' a lot. "Naturally!" he replied, with a mock-withering stare. "*Stupid* woman!").

We sat in one of the local pubs for a while before heading back, arriving in good time shortly after midnight.

*

During the Day for Doreen Valiente, I caught up with a few people and one of them was Marion Green, who is one of the first writers on actual witchcraft that I ever read. The result of our conversation, as I mention above, is that I will be doing some archiving for her over the next few weeks, as she has an immense amount of material accumulated over her years in the craft.

I told Marion that I have a doctorate, but not in history, and she replied rather dryly that the ability to read would probably prove sufficient. I did speak to Ronald about it, however, and he has given me some things to bear in mind.

I will be paid in cups of tea. Witchcraft runs on tea, as any reader of Mr Pratchett knows.

I'm increasingly coming to realise that this kind of thing has got to be done. It's not just my own interests, and Trevor's increasing academic immersion in the historical process, but I keep getting pointers. There were some people at the DV Day who have barely been seen in public over the last decade as they are very elderly indeed now. Whatever one thinks of Gardnerian and Alexandrian Wicca, in particular, we are still right at the start of a spiritual movement in this particular manifestation and it would be good to get a lot of this stuff documented. People are already doing this, of course, including the Boscastle Museum.

Comedy Toe

Anne's exhibition went very well, although on Day One I dropped the large piece of wood which is intended to secure the A-Frame to the building on my toe, which has now become a Comedy Toe. It has been so painful that I actually went to the doctor, who says it isn't broken ("Which toe is it?" "The large, red, shiny, balloon sized one?") Having a Comedy Toe makes me realise how much the dog treads on my feet with her enormous, starfish shaped paws.

Curses

Yesterday, a nicely-dressed middle aged woman came into the shop and, visibly gathering her courage, asked us if we could put her in touch with a coven. I said no, as the only teaching coven in Glastonbury has been run by a drug-dealing incompetent, namely Rat Girl, and the others don't advertise. I asked her why she wanted one, and she said she was looking for help.

Then she started to cry. She said she'd fallen in with a bad bunch of people and she thought they'd cursed her. She was very upset, and because I was in the middle of something and also, frankly, because we do get a lot of nutters, I took her down to

Jamie and asked him to deal with her. We get quite a few people who say they've been cursed, when what they mean is that they've had an argument with the neighbours etc, or have been inside a pyramid on a package tour... or something completely vacuous and born of watching too much Buffy.

The customer did not come back, but later Jamie came in and it turned out that she actually had been cursed. Jamie phoned a voodoo-practising contact in her home town, which is in the north, and asked him point-blank. "How did you know about that?" was the reply. Anyway, the woman's ex's new girlfriend apparently paid this guy £600 to have her magically killed, which is nice work if you can get it, I supposed. So Jamie has removed the curse (free of charge) and the customer is happy.

Ritual

There's a lot of it about. Some time ago the Dion Fortune reading group suggested that it would like to do an actual ritual as opposed to just the reading, since we've gone through a lot of Fortune's work. So I said I would do one, which needless to say I left until yesterday morning, in preparation for yesterday evening.

There is quite a lot of invocation in the ritual, which is a Golden Dawn rite and a basic element of a lot of ceremonial magical practice (this is the rite of which some would-be magus in the shop remarked, 'Yes, I know them well,' when mention of it was made and Jamie had to explain that it was a ritual not a group). I have done it before, but not led it. So I cobbled something together and then, when I got to the group, found that one of them had invited her new upstairs neighbour, who has been a practising kabbalist for eighteen years, is a leading light of one of the most respected kabbalistic groups in the country and has done more rituals than I've had hot dinners.

Anyway, I didn't fluff it, but nor did I do it properly. He was very kind about the whole thing.

Tonight we had another kabbalistic pathworking led by someone else, which focused more on the meditative side of things. It was interesting but slightly bolloxed up by my shoulder, which has suddenly decided to hurt.

Dartmoor

I drove down to a very misty Dartmoor yesterday to attend the Rivenstone festival: this is a small alternative music festival hosted on their property by Carolyn Hillyer and Nigel Shaw, who will be known to some of you for their music, art and workshops. This year featured a forum named Dream the Land, and I went down to read some of the late Rob Holdstock's work: a considerable honour to be asked, and it was good to represent someone who was my friend.

When I first came to the farm some years ago, I wandered up onto the moor and by a stream that runs through the property, I came across a mask in a small wood, a mass of twisted branches of oak. It gave me a start: it felt as though I'd wandered into one of Rob's novels and I remember thinking this at the time. I mentioned it to Carolyn and she said that they'd both been very inspired by Rob's work (I had a long conversation with Nigel yesterday about this – they did not know Rob, although they corresponded, and yet had much of the same sensibility). Yesterday, I found that a local (I assume) artist has created a set of the masks that appear in Lavondyss, and they're in an installation in a glade, along with a magnificent cloak of feathers. I spent some time there, and some time in the roundhouse, remembering Rob.

I did a selection of readings from Lavondyss, alongside one of the local farmers, who writes poetry, artist Dorrie Joy, and a local potter. There seems to be a very vibrant artistic community on the moor and it was good to be part of that, albeit temporarily. C and N have created a remarkable event: a small, non-commercial, well-run music and arts festival that many people return to again.

Happy Place

Will the 'responsible' parent kindly put that wailing little SHIT
out of my misery... With respect and love in a calm and reasoned
space. Happy place. Om...

October

Not Enough Demons

I have just found six demons that I thought were out of stock. They're little statues of Belphegor and Behemoth. They have been very popular. A lot of people think they are sweet (!), and one young lady asked me if one of them could be used to do magic in her office (this is one of those denizens of Hell whose speciality is flinging excrement at people, which it says on the little information card that helpfully accompanies him.) 'Whose excrement?' she asked brightly, and at that point I had to enquire as to whether she had ever done any actual magical practice. "No," she said, but appeared totally unfazed by the possibility that this might require something along the lines of an occult dirty protest. I talked her out of it, but you have to wonder what goes through people's minds.

*

Saw a guy wearing T-Shirt in the Cat & Cauldron with a message from my own heart – 'I love my country – it is my government I am afraid of'.

*

Living with a strange swampy smell, after Lily mistook pond weed for a solid surface in the ditch this morning. I really TRIED not to laugh, honest...

*

(*Since the events in Diary 1, I – Liz – was, rather surprisingly, elected Chair of the Glastonbury Chamber of Commerce. This was not an office that I particularly sought, and it was really a case of not ducking fast enough when someone else stepped back, at a rather exciting town meeting where people were invited to step out to the car park and insults were hurled. The Chamber under my incumbancy, which at the time of writing has now ended, was a lot more boring, but it will feature a little in these pages.)*

We might only be in October, but Christmas is approaching swiftly. Last night saw a series of meetings regarding the Chamber and the forthcoming Frost Fair, Glastonbury's annual Christmas/Solstice street fair. Actually, I lie: my colleague R and I had a two minute meeting standing in the hall of the leisure centre, since no one else turned up. This is typical of things about which people Feel Strongly. Immediately after the previous fair, which we did not organise, everyone turned up to the post mortem meetings and all were indignant and enthusiastic, but then the year wore on and enthusiasm has waned. So R and I said: *sod them, we will just do it ourselves*, and R has gone out and hired reindeer, sleighs, bands, organised road closures etc. Originally, I wanted wolves and a petting pen, but this was vetoed by the Mayor with – R and I think – a lamentable lack of risk and initiative. Although, as R remarked, "You'd probably just get people throwing swans into it."

The Chamber of Commerce, i.e. myself and R, vetoed a suggestion that we feature local didgeridoo players etc in the town square, and have got a rock band doing covers instead – currently Dire Straits. There are a couple of people here who have not yet recovered from going into a local pub last year, thinking that the bloke doing Mark Knopfler covers was really not bad at all, and then realising that he *was* Mark Knopfler.

*

Reading a copy of Pembrokeshire Life, which features a '100 years ago today' section, that includes a rugby forward who was assaulted in 1912 in the street by a female supporter of the losing team. He did not retaliate, which was probably lucky for her.

*

You could tell he wasn't from Glastonbury... Felt he had to explain to a Witchcraft shop owner exactly WHY he was dressed in a medieval Knight's chain armour...

*

Walking down the High St last night, I was suddenly accosted by St George, in full armour and a sword, who leaped out of the doorway of the George and Pilgrim Hotel, appropriately enough, exclaiming 'Ah! a damsel!'

I explained that I was not, however, in distress and St George disappeared.

*

Last night, we saw a couple who want us to handfast them in May. They're not actually pagan, but just like the idea of a handfasting. During the evening, the bride, who is Indian and in her thirties, confessed that her main ambition in life is to do a book binding and restoration course and 'make ill books better'. I nearly told her that if, gods forbid, she is dumped before the handfasting, *I'll* marry her, but thought this might sound weird.

Maximised

We have Whitby this weekend and the amount of stuff that needs to be done prior to Whitby (VAT return, accounts, mss appraisals and Chamber correspondence) has been piling up to the extent that I feel stretched in about fourteen directions. Finally managed to get details of a talk we're hosting next week up on Facebook and the person giving the talk just came in to have a chat about it.

"I am," he said, "somewhat maximised at the moment."

"I," I replied, "am maximised beyond the boundaries of my actual competence."

"Boundaries of competence," P remarked, "are best evaluated years in hindsight or years in advance, and rarely at the actual moment of their operation. It'll all be all right on the night."

*

Woman in shop: I just wanted you to know that I've come to town to live. I – am the GODDESS OF LOVE. [Observing that Jamie is looking at her dress, which barely conceals her exceptionally ample frame] Oh, I make all my own clothes.

Jamie [unfortunately in 'out loud' voice]: You'd fucking have to. [momentarily horrified], That is, I mean –

Woman: I'm sorry, dear, I'm a little hard of hearing. What did you say?

Jamie: WHAT A LOVELY DRESS.

Copycat Dogs Are Us
Cass managed to fall in the same ditch pond as Lily did two months ago. Except she is of course a lot BIGGER – so she stirred up the bottom mud as well... And she STINKS of it. I have to keep her in the shop all day. Joy...

Maximised Beyond Competence
Yesterday I distinguished myself by leaving money for a colleague on the counter, where anyone could nick it. I've spent last night, therefore, berating myself and being somewhat berated by my other half, it must be said, because someone apparently did. In the cold light of morn it appears that my colleague popped in and collected the cash herself, so no harm done, but that's not the point.

Resolving to do better, we packed the car for Whitby this evening, had a civilised drink in the G&P, returned in separate cars to an early night, whereupon Mr Jones, on returning with the rubbish bags from the shop, hurled them into the tack room, along with the car keys. Luckily the tack room has a light, but it took some time to find them.

I have suggested that it would add an extra frisson to the night if I simply fling the keys to the Jeep from an upstairs window into the bramble-infested front garden, but since I am likely to do something equally stupid between now and 4 a.m., which is when we're leaving, we have decided to leave well alone instead.

Wish us luck.

Whitby

We have just returned from Whitby and the Goth Festival – we took a stall up at the Spa, which is perched on the very dramatic West Cliff, opposite the Abbey.

We started out at 4.30 a.m on Thursday and arrived in Yorkshire by half past ten. It was a lovely day, so we drove down to Goathland (Heartbeat was filmed here, if anyone watches that) and followed the old Roman road on foot into larch woodland for a bit before heading into Whitby itself. We visited a number of the town's pubs over the weekend – it's an old-fashioned town and the first pub had a petition on the bar asking for support for Whitby's fishing fleet. We also admired Whitby's magnificent steam-powered bus.

Trade was very slow, but we managed to get out to the various other stalls of the festival and had plenty of time to people-watch. There were some stunning costumes – a high percentage of people in their sixties and even seventies, dressed in full Victorian gear. First prize from me went to an elderly lady in full mourning rig, and a steampunk couple (he was in copper armour with a whirring top hat and his partner was a balloonist of some description). Wandering around Whitby with all this going on was a lot of fun. I had lunch in a tiny cafe called Sherlock's, which did bear a close resemblance to the Baker St rooms, with added cake, and which was full of women in hats, buttoned boots and mobile phones. Ah, modern life.

We went to the Spa on both the Friday and Saturday evening, but alas, although I have dressed like a Goth for the last twenty-five years, I do not care for the music (there are exceptions – our good friends in Cauda Pavonis being some of them), so we hung out in the bar above a raging sea and caught up with people instead.

We stayed with some old friends in one of the nearby villages – great to see them and all their cats, too. Also excellent to visit folk singing friends on the way back. We decided to cut out the motorway as much as possible and headed back over the Peaks, having lunch in a place called the Lamb Inn (Derbyshire), which the wide-eyed barmaid informed me was 'ever so haunted.' Got back about six yesterday afternoon.

On Inevitability Theory –

Why is it that you get NO customers all morning, then as soon as you bite into the bacon & mushroom sandwich, the damned shop fills up with paying customers? Bless them...

Samhain Week

I'm famous for my trypning erors. I've just received a recipe for a Samhain punch bowl from Jamie, complete with what I fervently HOPE was a tryping error, or maybe an antique Carribean spellinge – I quote "tequilla, rum, archers and cocke'

*

It's been a busy week so far, with a lot of people in town for both the Day of the Dead Conference up at the Grail Centre, and the Faery Ball: some fabulous costumes last night for the latter. The George and Pilgrim has gone all out with the Hallowe'en decorations, which are a bit... interactive... for peace of mind: there's a thing hanging down the chimney which howls, thrashes and emits smoke if you go too close to it. We're inured to weirdness here, but even so... Good weather, but rather oddly mild for the time of year. Some of the trees around here are beautiful and we saw a flock of chaffinches on the bird reserve this morning, and met a sedate family of swans. Lots of ducks and geese flying over as well.

I took the dogs around the whole perimeter of the bird reserve today – lots of wild swans and a very tiny newt struggling gamely across the path. I've just been re-reading Steven Mithen's book about the post Ice Age and the alder carr and birch stands were laid down then: it feels like a very primitive landscape. There used to be people living here 4000 years ago and much further back in Cheddar, but alas, those people ate other people so not so much with the 'visiting the ancestors' thing. The weather is still glorious – not very cold, but bright.

New Member of the Household
...but not in a good way.

Lodger told me that other day that there is a large and rather smug rat in the attic. He has a friend, possibly about the size of a large cat given the noise that they make, and they are obviously teenage rats, because they get up about 10 pm, chase each other up and down and then go out, probably clubbing, to return around 4.

Also, the rat has stolen our friend E's lollipops, which she bought at Hallowe'en and kept in a bag: it hasn't eaten them, but it has taken them away, one by one. Somewhere in this house is a huge secret stash of lollipops...

*

Trevor just inadvertently locked a customer in the shop and went to get a cup of coffee.

She was so traumatised that she has bought two dresses (actually, she said she didn't notice until the dog started making meeping noises because Dad Gone).

*

Our elderly dog is going to have to be more closely confined. Halfway through the radio show, I looked up to see a disapproving policeman standing silently at the window like an apparition. This astonished me so much that I lost all power of speech and simply gaped at him. This isn't a good thing when you're live on the radio on air. Apparently Elderly Dog has been cavorting about in the road. We can't see how, because Dog appeared behind Trevor as the policeman was speaking and all the doors are closed, so either the copper let him in or Dog has taken to teleporting.

There was a piece in the paper today about a policewoman who got shot in the leg by an armed robber and set her Alsatian on her assailant. The dog, who is aptly named Chaos, bit her instead, in the arm. Luckily she was not badly hurt and the robber later turned himself in. This is what our Alsatian is like. If I set him on a burglar he'd just stare at me in dim bafflement and bat his enormous ears, although he might sit on the burglar's feet.

*

We went to see Robin Williamson in concert at the Assembly Rooms last night. The support was someone who won the local Bardic Gorsedd this year, and two young men named Will and Ed, who walk from place to place collecting folk songs. They've walked here from Canterbury. They did a great rendition of Sovay, but unfortunately were heckled from the audience. This being Glastonbury, and therefore Not Life As We Know It, the hecklers were a group of elderly women, who were stared at disapprovingly by some young punks in the audience.

Elderly Heckler (loudly): So *where* did you walk from, then? Where are you walking to next?

Audience member: What are you, their mum??

After Sovay, W and E did another, more experimental song:

W: We're not quite sure of this one, but let's try it, eh?

EH: You can do anything in Glastonbury!

Another audience member, with considerable sarcasm: So we've noticed.

*

After much cultural appropriation discussion earlier in the year, I could not help being thoroughly tickled yesterday by the presence in Cat & Cauldron, of a large Jamaican mama. How did I KNOW her origin? Well – from the tricolor flag tattooed on her arm... When I looked closer, said flag was actually a dress, for a little flying person. Underneath was a scroll containing the epithet – RASTAFAIRYAN – Thank you mama!

*

Has for the THIRD time this week returned a purse to its rightful owner – and no – NOT the same purse or person. PLease – let's be careful out there.

*

Customer: Shops like this encourage teenage girls into Satanism!
    Jamie: Yes, madam – and sodomy as well.
    Customer: I suppose you think that's funny!
    Jamie: No, madam. Actually I think it's quite painful.

*

My supper is in the dogs. I fell asleep after forwarding the essay, and awoke to the sound of paper and plastic being rent apart. A pound of VERY old cheese, half a black pudding, and some broccoli – they are so NOT sleeping in the bedroom tonight...

A la Ronde

We have had a lovely day down at A la Ronde on Exmouth today, where *(Now that would be) Telling*, the art installation constructed by Hayley Lock, for which I have done the text, was launched. Great to see the house again, and to take Trevor there, too – it has been a glorious autumn day. We had coffee, admired the house, I did a reading and then we walked around looking at Hayley's fascinating artwork. Both she and I have become quite inspired by this strange octagonal house and I doubt that this will be the last you'll hear of it from either of us.

After this, we drove to Seaton on the Jurassic Coast and had lunch, then walked up through the magnificently named Mutter Moor – beautiful beech woods and ancient droveways, overlooking the silver line of the Channel.

Special Snowflakes

At a wonderfully dull local govt meeting this afternoon, I revealed my recent difficulties and one of the women there said she used to work for a local book distributor. They found that one of their managers was nicking books and selling them on ebay.

When confronted, he told her that he'd expected a pay rise the year before, had not received same, and was just making up the discrepancy. S fired him and said he seemed quite surprised. A few months later, she received a reference request from Mulberry, who make bags. He'd applied for a job. So she rang him up and said, "Stealing? Fired for theft? Why on Earth are you asking me for a reference?"

She said he was quite put out, told her that he couldn't understand her attitude, and this was all in the past: meanwhile he had a family to support.

Imagicon

Science Fiction Convention time: I'm guest of honour at this year's Imagicon in Stockholm. After a very pleasant stopover in London and dinner in Camden at Belgo, I flew out on Friday morning and was met at Arlanda by Johan. We dropped my bags off at the hotel, then took the subway to Skarpnack and the the Kulturhus. I had a panel, meeting up with some Swedish authors – very interesting to hear their take on the genre and the state of publishing in Scandinavia. Later in the evening, Graham Joyce also showed up – good to catch up with him, too.

It was a good con – well organised and with some interesting panels. We managed to see a bit of Stockholm on Sunday night and on Monday one of the convention members, Tommy, very kindly offered to show me round the city. We went for a long walk along the sea front, ending up in the Old Town, the Gamla Stan, where to my delight there was a cannon ball embedded in a wall. It's a handsome city, very Hanseatic in feel. Towards the end of the afternoon Tommy had to catch his train to Malmo, but before he did so, put me on the bus to the Vasa Museum. This was fascinating – the Vasa is a warship, that sank in Stockholm Harbour on her maiden voyage in 1628. She'd gone less than a nautical mile. Seeing the ship, it is obvious why she foundered: top heavy and with inadequate ballast. She was raised in 1961. Looking at the boat is an eerie experience: it's a very Gothic museum.

After this, I caught the ferry back into the old town and had dinner in a nice quiet bistro before catching the subway back to my hotel, where I made some use of the sauna before retiring. The flight back next morning was uneventful, which is how I like flights.

In the Shop

B, who runs events here, hands me a selection of the latest leaflets.

Me: [pointing to leaflet] Ha! That's very amusing!

B: what is?

Me: that bit. Where it says 'entrance to the Farce, £1.'

B: [horror dawns across face]

Me: Ah... Look, tell everyone it was deliberate and you're just trying to keep them on their toes!

B: I've given out hundreds of these!

...then uttered name of small boy, who apparently has access to the computer and a very advanced reading age...

North Wales

Despite flu and sundry viruses, we have spent a lovely week in North Wales and the writing workshop went very well, I think, with some excellent writing, log fires, lots of chocolate and wine and a wander around Snowdonia. Wales is stunning at this time of year, with coppery beech and golden birch all along the mountain slopes and the bracken reflecting in the water of the lakes.

We had the traditional day off on Friday: some of the attendees went to Beaumaris, but Trevor and I drove to Denbigh to collect a sign for the shop, and subsequently went down via the Horsehoe Pass to Llangollen. Last year, I visited the house of the 'Ladies' of Llangollen, and I wanted to show it to Trevor: he was very impressed with the Mad Jacobean Oak Skillz of the Ladies and thought the house was delightful. This is an enchanting house, with every available surface covered in carved oak, and a smiling carved lion halfway down the bannisters. Each panel was covered with suns and moons and trees and faces, and the stained glass mosaics of the windows cast coloured shadows across the oak boards of the floor. On the way out, it turned out that a Tesco lorry had overturned on the A5, so we took the Dee valley road, which is about as wide as the car: everyone else had the same idea and there was rather a lot of reversing down steep bends. Anyway, we survived, and the Dee valley is glorious: stands of oak, fat cattle grazing in water meadows, and the rolling ruin-crowned hills all around.

On Saturday, we drove home via Machynlleth: a friend who is a longstanding occultist and writer had very kindly invited us to lunch. He is the only person I know who owns an ostrich. He used to own five, but the other four died from heart attacks caused by low flying jets – poor ostriches! We were asked not to open any doors in case a cat escaped – since this is a house with thirty two rooms, I will leave you to do the cat maths. I did let one out (fat and terrified). And I was sat on by a bull mastiff, the sort of dog who Wuvs Everyone. And there was a cockatiel...

We reached Gloucester about six and spent a pleasant family evening there, then rose early next morning and drove via Oxford to West Wycombe and an engagement at the Hellfire Club caverns. The churchyard at West Wycombe was a good place to spend the morning, with its chestnut trees and the Venetian-inspired church bearing its famous golden ball. We went into the caves about midday – very interesting. Francis Dashwood had the hill quarried out in order to provide employment for local people, and the caves are quite extensive, ending in a river crossing and a small inner temple. The estate is still owned by the family.

After this, we went to the George and Dragon in West Wycombe, which is a nice half-timbered village, and had lunch before heading home.

*

Lily has not been well during our absence, but seems to be better now. She stayed with the voodoo boys and Phineas the strange small cat last week, but they have forgiven her everything because she slipped her lead, charged down the road and was finally caught in the middle of a gastric episode of epic dimensions all over Exployee's doorstep. In the note that Trevor wrote for Jamie and Jack explaining about dog food etc, which he forgot to give to them and which I just found, I note that he suggests that they take Lily for a 'walk' outside that very address. It's as though she could read.

*

On the blossoming of a local star musician, I am for some reason feeling particularly proud of a young lady I do not even know that well. Congratulations to Lenny, who has quit her job to develop her musical career. Whatever comes of it, she will never regret getting an album out there.

Maman

Jamie has set up an altar in Witchcraft to Maman Brigitte, who is Baron Samedi's wife and apparently a kind of theological descendent of St Bridget/the goddess Bride, who came over to the Caribbean with the Irish and Scots. He did this last night but we're not sure whether she likes it or not, as the whole thing caught fire this morning (without candles). Apart from a fetish of Maman, nothing else is damaged.

November

Carnival

Carnival night was marked by the very sad and sudden death of one of the caretakers at the Assembly Rooms, who collapsed from a fatal heart attack (as another friend said, 'He went out surrounded by men in uniform. It would have made him happy'), way too young at forty. His funeral was yesterday, with a wake at the Assembly Rooms, after which a friend of ours fell down the steps. One of the local itinerants found him, couldn't wake him up... and so left him there, overnight. Those of you in the UK will know how cold it is at the moment. He was found this morning and taken to Frenchay, which is the head injuries unit. He survived, but it was touch and go.

A friend said, correctly, that it's like an Irish funeral – ending up either in a massive punch-up, or another funeral.

Voodoo Service

At the moment, we are hosting a weekend workshop in Glastonbury for a New Jersey-based Puerto Rican Houngan, H, who practices a combination of Dominican and Haitian vodou and Sanse, which I think is a form of Puerto Rican spiritualism.

I'm not called to this particular path and I don't know a lot about it, so I have not been on the workshop. H did, however, kindly invite both Trevor and myself to a service last night. Trevor is up to his eyes in exam revision at present, so did not attend, but I went along.

This started about 7.30 and went on until just before midnight. This kind of voodoo is apparently relatively informal, so we began by singing some chants and praising the *lwa*, and then it was basically a series of possessions of H and other people by various spirits, and consultations accordingly. It was a relaxed, pleasant atmosphere on the whole. I do not work in a tradition which involves full-on possession, and some of this was the dropping to the floor, heel drumming, screaming kind (some of the Petro fire spirits, I'm informed, come in fast and hard and leave just as abruptly). Most of it, however, was a lot calmer (luckily, as we did get a visit from one of the neighbours, who asked very mildly what all the shrieking and building-shaking was about, but when I explained he said simply that they did not mind as long as it didn't go on for too long. I did not, quite frankly, feel up to the task of explaining that an entity from Haiti felt the need to pogo).

I will not try to compress a four hour service into a diary entry, but the possession bit of it, which was most of it, was topped and tailed by Brav Gede Nibo, who is somewhat related to Baron Samedi (if I am correct, and I may not be), and who is a deity of the dead with the top hat and sunglasses. He is extremely funny and extremely rude (his advice to a rather disastrous acquaintance of ours was: "You ain't getting none! And that's because you're dried up down there! You know what you did, and that's why. I can't fix that! But I can do something about your knees.") All he said to me was that his wife is the spirit who works with me, which we knew, but it was interesting to have this confirmed.

The other three main possessors were an ancient Spanish spirit, whose name I cannot recall; Anaisa Pye, and Ogou Feray. Anaisa Pye is female, very flirty and funny (her handmaidens were a bit slow off the mark producing cigarettes, and she sat rolling her eyes in a 'God! WHY is this taking so LONG!' manner. Given that she was occupying a male body at the time, this was somewhat odd). She gave everyone advice (including, for me, some advice about Trevor's health: 'He's only a man, remember. And they... just don't cope so well.').

Ogou Feray, quite unexpectedly, took a liking to me and I can safely say that I have not, to date, had the experience of being violently patted on the head by a possessed man wielding a machete. He is a deity of war.

After all this, there was the aforementioned session with the Petro, Brav Gede Nibo returned, and we finished up.

So, racial/cultural factors. H is of Hispanic extraction and brought up in this tradition. Everyone at the service was white, although most of Jamie's clients at the moment are of Nigerian extraction from Bristol and London. Jamie is obviously not black, but they seem to have done a kind of racial sleight-of hand with him: he is, to the ladies who ring up, 'the white Creole gentleman.' Jamie has pointed out that he is in fact Welsh, despite training in New Orleans, to which they reply: "Yes! White Creole."

Voodoo seems to be the up-and-coming fashion in magic these days with people in their twenties. The voodoo societies whom Jamie has been in touch with don't seem to have a big issue with white practitioners, as they hold that everyone on the planet has a spirit with whom they walk and if the lwa choose you, no one human has much say in the matter (this is assuming that you actually make an effort to do it properly and not as some fashionable money spinner). This doesn't mean, obviously, that you should just take on another tradition because it's the cool thing to do.

Jamie is adamant that he doesn't want to be a houngan (priest) as it is very hard work indeed – far more so than being, for instance, a Wiccan HP.

The base issue is, I suppose, whether you consider the spirits of any religion to be real. As far as I am concerned, I do. There was no question that H or anyone else was faking, and I don't see how someone who is a complete stranger to you can give you information about your spiritual life which you've never actually divulged to another human being, unless there is something else going on. So for me, it is going to be a question of honour and respect, like being a guest in someone's home, or having them as a guest in yours. We stayed with a Jewish friend in NY a year or so ago and she very kindly invited us to do some ritual work for the spring equinox while we were visiting. It seems to me that you can honour someone else's tradition without pretending that you are a part of it.

November 11th

I was in Wells today, and had to collect some shoes that would, the shoe menders said, be ready in an hour. So I went into the cathedral – mainly, I must confess, to look for Christmas presents in the shop. There was, however, an Armistice service on, and so I went to it – quite a number of people from local regiments and their families. It was a short, crisp service featuring the last post and ended twenty minutes later. However, from the point of view of an occultist, rather than a Christian (it may well be from a Christian point of view as well, but I can't say), these moments of silence possess a resonant power and serve to connect you to your country and your people in a way that other rituals often don't. The magical community of Britain used silence and prayer throughout the war (cf Dion Fortune's account of the magical battle of Britain), as a magical act.

My father fought in the Mediterranean theatre, across Egypt and Lebanon, ending up at Monte Cassino. My uncles and grandfather also served. We are not a military family: everyone was a conscript and my father does not have a high opinion of the British Army. He does, however, consider it to have been a just war, given Nazi atrocities, which is more than one can say for the ones we are now involved in.

*

On a completely different note, Jamie has made a little song, which goes:

The wonderful thing about Lilypups,
Is that Lilypups are wonderful things.
Their heads are filled with concrete,
And their tails are made of springs.'

Lily has just nutted Trevor in the bridge of the nose and caused a massive amount of blood.

*

I am being punished by the Health Authority for missing an appointment at the local cottage hospital (one that THEY re-organised on me). I now have to drive forty miles to Taunton for my latest Post-Cancer checkup. Means I get lunch in the Quantocks though – so not all bad...

The Avalon Random Healing Generator
This is Jack and Jamie's idea. You take a colour, an animal, and a gemstone, and add the word 'healing.' Thus, we have:

Blue Dolphin Sapphire Healing.
Golden Bear Ruby Healing.
Silver Wolf Crystal Healing.

I bet we could sell these.

Once More onto the Beach, Dear Friends...
A long walk down Somerset lanes and then on the almost deserted beach at Brean Down. Huge trees thrown up onto the beach by the sea – shows how powerful the recent storms have been. Trevor found an old iron ship's nail. Stopped for a swift half at the Burtle and overheard the following immortal exchange:
    Man 1: She's moving, but she says that when she goes, she'll empty the septic tank.
    Man 2: So – she's taking all her shit with her, then?

*

Sonny, do not tell me you are eighteen and then go bright red when I ask you for ID if you want to look at my swords – it does nothing for your street cred...

*

Scene: Benedict Street, This Morning:

Jamie steps outside to find elderly woman driver shunting a Jaguar out of a parking space.

Jamie (and several other people) – remonstrate. Eventually woman gets out.

Woman: I'm disabled! I can park where I like!

Jamie: So is the owner of the Jag! [points to sticker on dashboard]

Woman: Let he who is without sin cast the first stone!!!

Jamie: How about Deuteronomy, chapter 8, verse 6 – Thou Shalt Not Shunt Someone Else's Car Out of the Fucking Way!

Woman: And look at you all, huddled outside doorways! Typical Glastonbury! Why don't you get a job?

Jamie and several other people: point out that they're outside *their own shops.*

Woman storms off, ranting, but returns an hour or so later to apologise and opine that 'maybe she shouldn't be driving.'

Maybe not.

*

Today in Witchcraft, a couple of people gave Jack less respect than he deserves. He knows more about goddesses than most people on this planet. Hecate is NOT anywhere described as a Crone in ancient literature, and any modern book you may have read is WRONG. If you know different, please do advise me of your sources, but otherwise do NOT call her Crone. She is not too happy about that.

Malefic Magic

Jamie got a very odd letter yesterday from Exployee accusing him of using 'malefic magick' against her. This is apparently because he walked past her house last week as she and her husband were coming out: instead of ignoring him, they both popped back indoors, like people on a Swiss clock. However, Exployee is convinced that we have cursed her and that Jamie is Doing Something in the churchyard, which her house overlooks.

For the record, we have not cursed her. We couldn't be bothered.

I think this is possibly projection, as some weeks ago, a friend who has also had trouble with Exployee looked out of her window one night as she was closing the curtains, about 2 a.m. and found Exployee standing across the road staring up at the house. So I suppose if Exployee does it, she thinks everyone else does as well.

We thus have the benefit of watching someone deteriorate under the weight of their own paranoia, without actually having to do anything except mind our own business.

Reburial

Not a universally popular viewpoint amongst pagans:

This is posted here for balance sometimes missing from such emotive subjects, and it summarises my position brilliantly, which is that scientists are actually showing great respect for the dead BY keeping these bones for future study, and trying to learn as much as possible about them.

If you favour reburial, I respect your opinion, but I expect mine to be completely respected in return, so please do not feel that you need to try and 'persuade' me, or presume, or suggest, that you speak for me when discussing your opinion with others.

A Gentleman of the Road

I had a long conversation yesterday with a guy called Paul, who has been around town for the last three years or so. He makes a living by painting shop fronts (as in, doing paintings of them, not the actual woodwork etc), and he is quite a good artist. He keeps all his paints on an ancient bicycle and sleeps rough in the hills outside Glastonbury. He has done so for years (I think he's about fifty). He looks pretty rough, but he's a nice guy and we quite often have chats in the pub.

We had a chat yesterday over coffee, and he mentioned the government's benefit cuts. They won't affect him, as he doesn't sign on. He said that a lot of people in Glastonbury have tried to persuade him to fake mental or other illness in order to claim sickness benefit, but he has refused, basically because he could see the way the system was going and doesn't want to be dependent on it, but also because he has an idea that faking mental health issues are likely to lead to real ones, and I am not sure he is wrong. A lot of people here do swing the lead, unlike some of the northern (or other) towns where there is genuinely no work. Pride also had a role, Paul said.

He has tried settling down and renting a place, but doesn't get on with that sort of life. I have known a few people over the years who have gone on the road – they are relatively rare these days. I think he may sleep in barns or on people's sofas in the very cold weather. It's a hell of a difficult life, but Paul doesn't complain.

Since I wrote this entry, P died unexpectedly, and is much missed.

Are You...?
Person in street: [going up to Jamie] Are you Sarah Brightman?

J: [who is tall, with shortish black hair, is twenty-four, and, er, is a man] Do I LOOK like Sarah Brightman?

Person In Street: I dunno.

The Strength of Your Love
T is watching NFL on the computer, complete with American jewellery adverts:

Advert: Surround her...with the strength of *your love...*

Me: Are you going to surround me with the strength of your love, dear?

Trevor: [makes one of those wavering hand gestures] Meh.

*

Will be attending a book signing by a real Racing hero, champion trainer Paul Nicholls, and a pub lunch thrown in. My idea of a perfect day.

Ditcheat

We ran away today and went to a book signing at lunchtime, at the Manor Inn at Ditcheat. The signing was on behalf of racehorse trainer Paul Nicholls, who is currently training jump racing superstars Kauto Star, Denman, and Master Minded. We were slightly overdue as a result of getting stuck behind the yard's late morning string: a dozen beautiful horses, swaying down the lane.

Nicholls always comes across as a pleasant and unpretentious man and this was borne out at the signing. I bought his book (autobiography) as a Christmas present for T, who asked him about Master Minded, who recently broke a rib. Liz also broke a rib some while back, Trevor informed him, although I did point out to Nicholls that I am almost certainly somewhat less expensive than Master Minded.

We have a conversation with some people down from Shropshire and then came back via the Red Lion on the way to Glastonbury. The Manor Inn is lovely, but you need to book.

It's a typical winter afternoon – a thin blue sky, steely clouds, dripping bare branches. A good night to be indoors with a log fire and a chicken roasting in the oven.

Something Nasty in the Churchyard

Halfway through the day, a very aggressive man appeared in Witchcraft. It seems he is Exployee's next door neighbour, by the church.

He got off to something of the wrong foot by trying the big city 'hard man' act with Trevor, who simply replied wearily, "Look. I come from South London. I know people who are bigger and harder than you. So behave." Whereupon, he did, coming up to the upper shop and introducing himself with the words "I think I have upset your husband." He repeated this several times. "*Have* I upset him?" (This is exactly the sort of man who will then turn round and criticise women for being 'emotional.')

Trevor apparently told him, "Go and see my partner. I'm nice. She'll tear you to shreds." However, I exerted maximum charm and eventually Neighbour uncrossed his arms. The upshot of all this is that Neighbour says:

– Exployee is 'mental' and recently gave him a smack in the face when he was halfway up a ladder (!). I forget why: he did explain, but it was so trivial that I have forgotten. "I couldn't hit her back, because she's a woman," he remarked, with what I consider to be entirely misplaced gallantry, as Exployee is six foot tall, built like a brick shithouse, and would flatten the average bloke. I'd deck her, if someone got me a box to stand on. Jamie suggested that I simply erect a ladder outside her house and stand on it, holding a baseball bat.

– he has CCTV footage of Jamie engaging in the heinous activity of, er, walking past the house on the pavement, which he won't release to anyone, including Exployee, without a police warrant.

– Neighbour has, in fact, installed £6K's worth of surveillance equipment on his tiny terrace house because, although he lives in a quiet backwater of a small Somerset country town, he appears convinced that he is in fact inhabiting the centre of, say, downtown Chicago. And the government is out to get him, apparently. I was going to ask about his tinfoil hat, but thankfully reason prevailed.

*

My Mother has won the Spanish Lottery! 985,950 Euros! Excellent news – I'll pay the £3000 bank fees of course, but I'm not sure exactly how we are going to get it to her, as she DIED

IN 2004, you fucking offensive morons...

...Let It...
...and it did.

Woke up to a white world this morning. Since the Shetland has been confined to quarters in the orchard after his last escape attempt, Trevor put him in the barn with plenty of hay and fresh water. This was treated with contempt and the appropriately named Snowy has now vanished against a backdrop of whiteness in his field, after we'd stopped up any likely gaps.

Having done this, and having a day off, we've had a cookathon: chilli oil, homemade bread, colcannon, cauliflower cheese, game stew and a sponge cake. I'm intending to resist the temptation to do any work this afternoon and just read recipe books instead.

London
We met up in London on Saturday for the first Clarke jury meeting, which took place in a restaurant in Chinatown. Because the train is now too expensive, I caught the bus – it's a longer trip, but leaves from the middle of Glastonbury and drops off at Victoria, so couldn't be more central for either. It's a pretty run through Bath and the little villages of the Mendips: I saw a big red dog fox in a snowy field, and someone had written 'Merry Xmas' in huge letters in the snow.

London was packed – when our meeting was over, I walked from Soho through Trafalgar Square, stopping off at the National Gallery, and then down through London to Harrods, which was an absolute heaving mass of people. Lovely windows, though, and the food store is always fun even though I never buy anything in there. I love London at this time of year.

Self-Policing
First shoplifter of the Christmas season (that we're aware of), a sixteen year old who tried to sneak a pair of earrings up her

sleeve.

Jamie has apprehended her with the company-approved shoplifting policy: "Fucking put them back or I'll break your legs."

Result: earrings still in our possession and a terrified teenager.

*

Jamie has just had a slight difference of opinion with a customer in a rainbow knitted hat and a purple poncho who remarked that Glastonbury was full of Love, which beat out across the world, and the wonderful thing about it was that everyone in it Loves one another. As you know, this is not precisely the terminology I would use to describe the inhabitants of this town, many of whom can barely restrain themselves from punching each other in the face every morning as a kind of ritual greeting.

Jamie said so, and was treated to a lecture on Love and his own negative attitude, which would, I quote, 'ensure that he dies young'. Jamie replied that he would rather go young, virile and in a pool of his own blood than ancient, senile, and in a pool of his own piss, at which the customer was rather taken aback and left.

Sheep

I was due to go to Gloucester today and see my cousins on a pre-Xmas visit, so was wearing an ankle-length skirt and a smart sweater.

We were going to walk Lily and Cass down the lane as usual, but Lily saw sheep (which she has seen several times before) and took off out of the car – straight into the sheep field, and straight for a woolly old ewe. Trevor ran after her, shouting, and I ran after Trevor. We went right through a drainage ditch, in which we both fell flat on our faces, because, I have to tell you, a long skirt is not ideal when you are trying to sprint after a puppy with long legs.

I don't want to fall into a drainage ditch again.

We eventually collared Lily, who was walloped. Cue several

passing 4x4s, all of whom slowed to get a good view of a man beating a dog in the middle of someone else's sheep field, and a shrieking woman who was soaking wet.

The woolly old ewe is all right, thank God. By the time we caught up, she was staring at Lily with an air of mild contempt: *what was that for?* I then drove home, changed, went to Gloucester, had a nice time with my family and came back to a civic meeting at six, only to encounter a major accident on a quiet country lane which obliged me to take a detour of several miles.

*

Happy dance! I get to do Mr Scrooge today! Liz & Jamie are putting up the Yuletide Tree in The Magick Box – herrumph. Blasted nonsense. Bah humbug. For those visiting this weekend – there is an EMBARGO on Yule stock in all our shops until AFTER December 1st – you have been warned...

December

Mediaeval Baebes

I was teaching yesterday so went from Bath to Gloucester to have dinner with my family and go to a MB concert at Gloucester Cathedral. It took ages to get through Bath, which is a nightmare to drive in at the best of times.

However, the concert was very good and featured what might be the only song about female genitalia ever sung in the cathedral: it was in old Welsh, though. The cathedral is an ideal place for it, with its huge Norman pillars and creamy stonework. The cloisters (scene of some of the Harry Potter movies) were ethereal. There was a big Christmas tree with pale sparkly lights. When the lights were turned down the whole building was filled with shadows, like a huge ship sailing into the winter dark.

There is also a hilarious Nativity scene made out of papier maché, featuring a Gloucester Old Spot pig and a stout Joseph in wire rimmed spectacles.

Frost Fayre

It is a cold and Frosty morning – ideal for the Glastonbury Frost Fayre! Reindeer, chestnuts, Morris dancing, Hog Roast. A TRADITIONAL Fayre.

This went very well. There were a few hitches – mainly the logistics of siting stalls which were larger than expected, and some trouble from the dropouts who cluster around the Market Cross (as usual). Apart from this, however, it all went smoothly and the committee are now pleased and relieved.

R and I did realise, halfway through the afternoon, that we had neglected to find Santa a costume. Thank God for Proper Job, where you can buy a Santa outfit for a fiver!

But the reindeer and sleigh were lovely, the music was good, the food stalls were excellent and my week was made by the sight of the Mayor arm in arm with Witchcraft's resident fairy, complete with pink sparkly dreadlocks. She said he was very kind and kept asking questions as they went up the High St. ('Where are you from, my dear?' 'Fairyland!' 'No, I mean, really?' 'Fairyland!').

*

And the next negative comment from any trader regarding the Frost Fayre will be returned with the sharp end of a Christmas tree in a painful place. Well done to the Chamber of Commerce.

Apples

The bags of windfalls were supposed to go up to the cider farm two weeks ago, but our old dog's death, on the day we were going to do this, and Trevor's subsequent hand injuries, put a hitch in things. Poor old Tara had a seizure and bit through Trevor's finger: she was a Rottweiler. (He still has the scars).

*

A raw but thankfully dry start to the day, and the sad duty of laying Tara to her rest. The other three dogs are very quiet. They miss her.

Actually it was more like submerging Tara than burying – the water table rises very suddenly at this time of the year and after taking thirty gallons out of the hole it was clear it was filling just as fast. So I got the last laugh after all. She HATED getting wet. Rust in peace, Baggage...

*

So, apples have had to wait until this morning – I got up at first light, then went out and started tying up the bags (with some hemp string we bought because it looked stout – it breaks at the drop of a hat and proved totally useless). Round two: locate aid of baling twine with aid of Trevor, tie up bags again (Trevor did most of this), then, with the sterling aid of our lodger, load them into the Landrover (Lodger did all of this bit). They are now up at the cider farm and we are nursing various apple-related injuries (sacks of frozen apples are not easy to shift on a frosty morning) and are all rather dirty.

The redwings, thrushes and fieldfares have already descended in force to finish off the remaining windfalls, so they have food in this bitter weather, and we get rid of the rest of the crop by spring.

I walked the dogs briefly – there is a lot of black ice on the back roads, making it like a skating rink – then came into town. Trevor passed someone's car in the ditch. We have no snow, and it's normal winter conditions, but I don't want to go further than I have to today, so will not be druiding in Bristol tonight.

Instead, we will follow the custom that Trevor has done for the last twenty years and pour a ceremonial glass of cider over the orchard gate before closing it, and doing a small Solstice ritual in the orchard itself.

*

You'd think everyone would be too busy before Christmas, but no. The rumour mill churns merrily away. The latest is that Jamie and Jack have bought Witchcraft Ltd, and also another shop which does not belong to us. They have, however, allowed Trevor and I to stay on and work for them because – wait for it! – we are all involved in a black magic Lodge, along with a couple of other people. Jamie and Jack are training us in the Occult, apparently.

I'm assuming that this originates with Exployee, but it's being disseminated by one or more of the local priestesses.

The more worrying issue is that someone has written to the Inland Revenue accusing one of our staff members of not declaring income. She is in fact completely legitimate and can prove it, and so can we as everything goes through our accountants. Again, the most likely candidate is Exployee, who has a history of poison pen letters, including one that she circulated around the bookshop where she worked that was really old school: letters cut out of the newspaper. She rather blew this by then telling several people that she was responsible, which kind of negates the whole 'anonymity' thing.

The Holy Thorn

The darker news this week has been the damage done to the holy thorn tree on Wearyall Hill. This tree, and its siblings, are said to have been taken from an original tree which sprang from the staff of Joseph of Arimathea. Whatever one thinks of the truth of the legend, it's a lovely story, and whenever I go to the supermarket I have looked up at the little tree on its hillside, and thought of the legend. On the day that twigs were taken from a sister tree in St John's churchyard, to be sent to the Queen for her Christmas Day dinner table (an annual tradition of long standing), the Wearyall tree was vandalised overnight, sawn down to a stump. The town is furious, and upset. The tree may survive, but this is not the point. If it was simple vandalism, it's appalling, and if it was a protest of some kind, it has badly backfired. No one has claimed responsibility.

We're Dreaming of...

Woke up to a white world again – the orchard looked beautiful in the early morning sunlight, but it is now grey, cold, and continuing to snow. Trevor and I went into town, walking the dogs en route (Lily was so excited by the snow that she broke into a field and chased some cows – NOT admirable), but by this time the Jeep was fishtailing all over the road. This is not welcome, given that there are deep drainage ditches on either side, so we decided to go home. Staff and colleagues were going to man the shop up until the point where the weather became untenable.

They are talking about more snow tonight. Meanwhile, we are

holed up indoors with a log fire.

*

A stunning day – clear, cold, and snow-silent, with a fiery sunset and moonlight on the apple trees. We managed the ascent of the north face of Glastonbury High St, but trade has been badly affected (you can't blame people). I will be dealing with web orders tomorrow.

Death Eater Upgrade
Our friend G, who works as a movie extra, has had to head back north after a summons to the latest Harry Potter shoot – he has been upgraded from Death-Eater to parent, although we feel that this is not an upgrade.

*

FINALLY got one of the three dead cars as far as the garage, which means actually NO beer in the G&P arfter all. Sorry guys – I realise what a dent that puts in the weekend takings – hopefully the 175 druids coming to town will go some way to matching the lost consumption...

Earlier that same day – Attn OBODies gathering today for their Winter Assembly – please leave SOME beer in George & Pilgrims. I'm trapped in the office till 17:00!

Solstice Eve
It was snowing when we got up this morning, around 8, and continued throughout the morning. Our staff member walked in from the next town, which is a couple of miles. Someone we know overturned the car last night and a lorry jackknifed on the main road into Glastonbury, allegedly demolishing someone's front room.

I have been working on various things from home today, but have just walked down to the back field to take a bucket of water to Snowy, who has made a little horse nest under some blackthorn. He has a perfectly good barn, with straw, which he hates. The sky is a leaden, yellow-grey and it looks like there is more to come. The trip out to the shop was useful, as we discovered that a neighbouring house, which has a small farm shop attachment, also sells logs and kindling. But it goes to show why it is vital to use the local shops – which we do in non-emergencies. If they go, then you're left with no support structure and for the old people round here, that's critical.

The central heating has now kicked in properly and the house is no longer freezing. Since it is supposed to reach –26 tonight in some places (probably the Cairngorms and not Somerset, but even so, I am thankful). We did not get much above –3 yesterday.

For those of you who celebrate, a happy Solstice. I love this snowy world but I will not be sorry to see the return of the sun!

Happy Solstice

Beat the bounds this evening with a lantern. It is very quiet and still out there, apart from the sudden unnerving rush of snow cascading out of the ash trees. Easy to tell where the local badgers have been choosing for their wee place, however! I have heard owls regularly throughout the autumn, but not tonight.

I don't know what the temperature is but it doesn't feel that cold: then again, I was walking fairly briskly. No sign of the moon so I think any chance of seeing the eclipse is probably out. When I came back, we libated the orchard with cider brandy. And are now libating ourselves with the same thing.

Christmas Eve

The dog, who was unusually active last night, turns out to have broken into a bag of mince pies, eaten all of them, then had explosive diarrhoea all over the study carpet. And the chair.

We are working this morning, but will shortly be closing the shop to convene in the George and Pilgrim, before heading home. Cooking a Somerset pork roast has become traditional on Christmas Eve, and neither Trevor nor myself like to go out as the pubs turn into mayhem after about 4. I shall probably embark on the traditional Christmas read of *The Dark Is Rising*.

Vignette

The scene: a kitchen in Somerset. The cat is having his tea. I am on my way back from feeding the tortie sisters, to find that Cass has shouldered Sid out of the way and is eating his food.

Sid: mum, MUM, she's eating my tea!!!

Cass: [who knows this is wrong] ooo, sorr-eeeee, [cringes] [runs]

Me: THAT IS NOT YOUR DINNER!

[aims kick at dog's backside. Other foot slips on the doormat and I am deposited flat on my back on the flagstones with a yell]

Trevor: [emerging from peaceful NFL watching in the living room to investigate the yell, to find me lying blinking on the kitchen floor, surrounded by animals peering down at me.] What the fuck are you doing?

We have all been sent to our baskets.

Ironically, we have been extremely careful outside, given the ice and snow. Clearly it is within the home that I need to be careful.

Flood

I was supposed to have a day off today, but Trevor went into the shop mid-morning and came back about half an hour later to say that water was pouring through the ceiling and the floor was already several inches deep. We raced back into town, and he was not exaggerating – sheets of water cascading through the ceiling. A plumber friend was, thank God, available and he came over and shut the water off. We had to take the floorboards and one wall up to find the offending pipe, in the dark, as we did not dare switch on the lights.

With the help of Jamie and Jack, we bailed out the ground floor with plastic boxes and got rid of the worst of it, and then I went to the supermarket and hired a Rug Doctor, which has been surprisingly efficient when plugged into the one non-affected socket. The clothes have mainly escaped, and so have the herbs, which are in plastic bags and boxes, and anything else can be dried off. We have, I think, got off lightly, but could certainly have done without this. I doubt we will be alone – the county is thawing fast and there is heavy rain at the moment, so flooding is going to be a real issue.

*

Oh no! Lily pup is has gone astray. We know her reading habits. We found a copy of PC Monthly on the stairs. The shame of it – what have we done to deserve one of our dogs becoming a GEEK...?

January

Happy New Year

The dishwasher has broken down. The door of the washing machine has stuck with a load of laundry inside. Lily has thrown up on the carpet and I have just trodden in a large pile of dog shit while putting seeds out for the birds. We have two cars off the road, with brakes and clutch respectively, and the recently 'mended' Jeep may be ailing as well.

It is very cold here – I saw a string of wild swans flying into a clear red sunset this evening, one of the moments where I realise just how beautiful this region is. There are peewits on the water meadows and this morning T and I saw a heron perched on someone's gable, and a small white egret in one of the rhynes.

We also have a small sparkly horse. True to his Shetland origins, Snowy hates it when it's hot, but despite having a perfectly adequate barn to go into, prefers to stand out in the cold and on Saturday was covered in glittering frost.

Snow

We'd made an arrangement that if it started snowing, I'd come back into town and collect Trevor. Out in the orchard, a few flakes started coming down, so I kept an eye on it, messaged him and set out – by the time I got out of the back door, the snow had increased but there was still a thin line of wintry blue-green sky over the Tor. By the time we'd got out of the shop and on the road, it was as though someone had emptied an eiderdown over the landscape.

Just in time for Twelfth Night, which is either tonight or tomorrow, depending on how you count (I treat it as the sixth).

So I have said a sad goodbye to the Christmas tree, taken down the decorations and cleaned the house. Not a bad day to treat the snow as an excuse and hole up with various pieces of work.

*

Customer (from S Wales): 'E's got his court case on Monday, see, for the drugs, and I was wondering if you could do anything to 'elp 'im, because he didn't do it. Well, he did, but he didn't, if you see what I mean.

    Jamie: Pleading 'not guilty'?

    Customer: That's the one!

Occult Conference

We hosted the first Occult Conference in Glastonbury yesterday, organised by Jamie and Jack, and overall it went very well. We have had Hellfire Club Books to stay, in the form of E and C. E gave book binding demonstrations and brought down a lot of stock (all leather bound, gold stamped, marbled end papers etc: just lovely work if you are a book geek, which, needless to say, we are).

There were a number of other book dealers there – Hadean Press (Erzebet is published by Prime, as well) and Scarlet Imprint. We had talks on various matters, including Graeco-Roman 'voodoo' dolls, Babbalon, Goetic Magic and Hermetics.

In the evening, we had three bands: Anniversary Circle, Cauda Pavonis, and the magnificent Eileen Daly and the Courtesans, plus cuddly tiger. I have not met Eileen before, but she is delightful – one part Dickensian waif, one part scream queen, one part Kate Bush. She starred in vampire flick Razor Blade Smile.

The only issue with the conference was that one of the speakers took exception to something that another had said, and punched him. Trevor was obliged to separate the battling occultists on the steps of the Town Hall. Needless to say, the assailant will not be invited to speak at next year's conference, or indeed anything else that I am involved in ever again.

*

Odd requests are common in Glastonbury – but this one takes some beating – 'Have you seen my Dragon? He is purple and green'...

*

What at least one friend thought about my enthusiasm for blogs & why I wasn't getting my homework done –

Isn't it about time you came online to tell us that you haven't got time to come online and tell us that you are too busy to be online? Must be at least a few hours since you did that!

Save our Libraries

This has been very much on our minds here in recent weeks. Glastonbury has mounted a huge campaign to save our town library from closure – a library that is well-used and is host to many different services. It looks as though the campaign has been successful – which is obviously great news. But the campaign was founded on the principle that Glastonbury did not want its library to be saved at the expense of another one, and so the fight goes on.

Libraries have been a big part of my life, both as an academic, and as a student. When I was a teenager, back in the 70s and early 80s, visiting the local library was a treat. I found Andre Norton, Jack Vance, Isaac Asimov, and Ray Bradbury. I found Miss Read and Dorothy Sayers. I found too many authors to mention – authors whom I still read today and who are central to my career as a writer myself. And, of course, my own books are in libraries throughout the UK.

Green Woman

Because Glastonbury is what it is, and because a lot of people come here in search of something, we sometimes get customers who are in difficult circumstances. Neither Trevor nor myself are trained counsellors, but we have been through a gamut of experiences that at least allow us to understand, to some extent, where people are coming from.

Last week, a very nice American couple came in and were interested in a green woman – it's a ceramic plaque, to hang on the wall, and was made by a woman in Yorkshire who got tired of all the green men. It's a round, rather beautiful face, surrounded by leaves. The couple were fascinated by her, and asked me if they could bring some friends in to look at it today (they haven't shown up yet). The face, they said, is identical to the face of the young daughter of the other couple, who hanged herself last year from an apple tree.

You encounter other people's stories, and you deal with them as best you can.

Kitten

Henry is not a Christmas kitten. But we did take a look at the rescue site on Wednesday, and I called on Thursday. He is, I was told, seven months and very timid, but we were welcome to come and see him today, which we did. He is a tiny black imp.

Woman at Cattery: He is very shy! His brother was very confident, but this one...

[We walk into cat cage]

Henry: Helooooooooooo!

Woman: He's extremely timid...

Henry: [grabs sleeve, start biting thumb]

WAC: He will neeed a lot of care..

Henry: [upside down] I'm standing on my head. Because. I. Am. Incredibly Cool! LOOK!

WAC: He's a shy little chap...

Henry: [pokepokepoke] Look! Now I'm attacking my amazingly fierce back leg! And now the six foot bloke you've brought with you! I can take him any day! Because I Haz The Amazing Fierceness!

WAC: Er... Have you rubbed yourself with catnip? [this is verbatim, BTW]

Me: [modestly] No, cats just like me [this is only partly true]

Henry: And now... I will fall off the chair! Because I meant to! Wheeee!

WAC: [uncertainly] I've never actually seen him behave like this... He will need to be Brought On.

Me: [thinks, but does not say] Any more bringing on, and Henry will be leading a tank regiment into France by Thursday.

(Eight months later, Henry rules the household with an iron paw; he has been Brought On marvellously).

My True Name

Last night, Trevor and I went to the pub for a quick drink and a couple were sitting next to us – she was blonde, in her thirties, American and had that sort of breathy delivery that signifies the true believer of the Californian New Age. The bloke didn't say a word but he had that thought bubble over his head that says clearly, 'Really, I'm just listening to this shit so I can get into your knickers, so I'll just smile and nod.' The bits I overheard were chakras, spirit guides, energy... the usual. I didn't pay much attention because I was involved in a conversation of my own and only tuned in when Trevor went to the bar.

This morning, in the shop:

Blonde New Ager: [walks in] Hi! I've been channelling the spirits and they've told me I can do a trade? If you do a tarot reading for me, I'll give you your true name.

Jamie: [*thinks: nice try, madam!*] FANTASTIC! Because I've been searching for my true name since the dawn of time. You're on!

Blonde New Ager: [perks up]

Jamie: However, because I get this a lot, I have to ask you for the birth certificate that goes with it.

Blonde New Ager: Sorry?

Jamie: I get this all the time. So I'll need proof. Where is it?

Blonde New Ager: Uh... the spirits didn't give it to me. I'll have to channel it.

Jamie: so you DON'T have my true name!

Blonde New Ager: [flails] Uh, well, uh, the spirits said they'd give it to me during the tarot reading.

Jamie: Look, you come in here, WITHOUT MY BIRTH CERTIFICATE, and then you lie to me! Just like yesterday! And the day before!

Blonde New Ager: [blanches] But I wasn't in here yesterday!

J: You most certainly were!

Blonde New Ager: Was I?

Jamie: Yes!

Blonde New Ager: But I need a tarot reading...

Jamie: And I need my true name, but since I've been searching for that for aeons, and you've only been wanting a reading since Thursday, I think I take priority!

Blonde New Ager: Um, can I look round?

Jamie: Certainly. It's a shop. And I've put your candles aside.

Blonde New Ager: My...?

Jamie: The candles you ordered when you were here yesterday!

Blonde New Ager: I think I'd better go.

Game-tastic

No snow down here, although the Mendip hills are white again. We've had heavy, sleety rain today but then a late golden light and an inky sky, turning to a very wintery sunset.

There seem to have been a lot of shoots around here – I keep hearing guns when I go out to the field and people keep giving up pheasants. Trevor plucked a brace last night, and I just did another brace, for the freezer. Sid the cat thinks that this is the most exciting thing to have happened in this household for weeks and paid close attention, occasionally head-butting me in the leg to remind me that he was there. Then he stole some leftover Chinese takeaway, because Sid has wide tastes.

But Very Polite...

A pleasant man who looked like a ceremonial magician (goatee beard, black t-shirt, pierced ear, and who was also enormous) walked into one of the shops a little while ago:

CM: Excuse me, but does Exployee work here?

Jamie: I'm afraid she was fired.

CM: Good! May I ask why?

Jamie: [tells him]

CM: hmmm.

Jamie: could I ask why you're looking for her?

CM: Actually, I have a message for her. Is there any way someone could pass it on?

Jamie: Yes, we know where she lives. What's the message?

CM: [still very politely] Just that it's difficult to practice the left hand path when someone's cut your fucking hands off.

It looks, however, as though Exployee may now have moved, presumably to embark on the rest of what may turn out to be an exciting life.

She's On Fire...

The bank – Lloyds – keep ringing me about something fairly minor. It's one of their offshore divisions, and when I actually spoke to them, some weeks ago, they asked me for my security details. I gave them, but they could not verify them – God knows why. They asked me to contact my branch. I wrote to them. I've also spoken to my branch here and they have promised to sort things out.

Since then the branch have kept calling, and I have kept refusing to speak to them, because if they can't verify my details, there is no point. They keep ringing the shop as well, and it turns out that J has become creative and has told them variously that I am dead, have been run over, am in the back smoking crack, have been arrested and, this morning, that I cannot come to the phone because I am on fire.

Is That Your Puppy?

Later on, in Witchcraft:

Jamie [looks up from behind counter to find teenage dominatrix with slave on leash]: Yes?

Teenage Dominatrix: [poses, smirks]

Jamie: Aw, is that your puppy?

Teenage Dominatrix: Er –

Jamie: Did you ask if you could bring dogs in here?

Teenage Dominatrix: No, I –

Jamie: In that case, you can leave him behind the counter. We have kittens. Also candy. [crooks finger in beckoning gesture] Come on.

Slave: [starts actually to go behind counter]

Teenage Dominatrix: [annoyed] WE'RE LEAVING.

*

Needless to say, I have seen none of these people, although we both have suffered from Incredibly Rude Goth Girl, a redhead who interrupted me halfway through serving another customer and who shoved a woman in a wheelchair out of the way, this afternoon.

BTW, for those who doubt my veracity, I direct you to Google 'slave's outing at the supermarket', here (the dominatrix is not the one referred to above, but one of our nicer acquaintances). Since this is Glastonbury High St, 'you look lovely' is an entirely normal reaction.

*

Somerset levels nearly had a frost this morning. Lily the Artist excelled herself. Latest composition – Duck-down cushion explosion on red.

*

Lodger and girlfriend have had to move out. Like many young people, they can no longer afford independent rent and have had to move back in with Mum and Dad. So we have advertised the flat with the local estate agents (the very strange Ralph Bending), whom I see have actually got it advertised as 'dirty but nice two bedroom hovel out in the sticks.' Amazingly, given their infamous marketing, RB do a roaring trade in rentals and we have already got viewings arranged: one arrived this morning and turned out to be a customer.

Apparently there was this conversation in the estate agents:

Estate Agent: So – you're self-employed. What is it that you actually do?

Flat Viewer: It's alternative.

EA: OK, does that mean a therapist, or...?

V: I've been a fairy. For the last 20 years.

EA [internal thought process: don'tlaughdon'tlaughdon't LAUGH!] Okaaaaay...

Anyway, I had forgotten to mention to RB that we would prefer not to take members of the fae, especially royalty, but I have now had to have this conversation and we will see what results. However, FV has offered six months' rent up front, which will be fine as long as it doesn't turn to leaves in the morning.

End of January

It's been cold and grey in the main, but some days have had that odd quality of light which suggests spring and on Tuesday there was an extraordinary sunset, gold and pink and lilac: I remember similar pink-gold evening skies in Hong Kong, but such an intensity of colour is unusual here.

We've made a number of visits to the Bird Reserve this week. Our walk on Tuesday saw us circled by a pair of swans, flying round and round with huge slow strokes of their wings. There are flocks of them out on the Levels, pottering about in the waterlogged fields. We also saw a nuthatch, and cormorants, perhaps driven inland by the weather.

The field opposite the house now has nearly thirty lambs –

this must be a breed that lambs early, but my mother recalls a variety of sheep that give birth in November, so they do vary quite a lot. They are as sweet as lambs always are and head-butt one another. When I let the dogs out last thing, I hear bleating and usually a voice shouting 'Where's he gone now? Where are you?' The lot of the sheep farmer in winter...

Imbolc is at the weekend. I'm not sure what we'll be doing for it, although there are events on Monday and I'll probably try to attend a couple of them. I always love this festival. We put Bride in her 'bed' in the window of one of the shops for the duration – an elderly Scots woman came in some years ago and reminisced about making a Bride doll. Her brother used to kidnap it and hold it to ransom, she said. Typical of small boys but Bridget seems to have a broad sense of humour in all the folklore about her, and I suspect she did not mind.

*

It is a reflection of the seasonal downturn that we are losing a couple of staff soon now, and we are not going to replace them. Yet I have already had THREE people in today either looking for work and/or looking to move here so they can teach crystal therapy for a living. Sigh...

February

London

I went up on the dawn bus to London on Thursday, to deliver a talk at Treadwell's bookshop in Bloomsbury on Thursday night. A good day in town, mainly spent in the British Museum, and then I met F and E who very kindly took me to dinner at an excellent Vietnamese place off Goodge Street. The talk went well and seems to have been well received – this was on Glastonbury and the Avalonians of the early 20th C.

On Friday I met up with my friend T for lunch in Borough Market – I don't know why I haven't discovered this outstanding market before, but since she suggested meeting at London Bridge, and since I was early, I went into Southwark Cathedral, which is rather lovely, and then into the market – magnificent displays of cheese, artisinal bread, fish and meat from around the country. I bought some lamb chops from the Rhyg estate, which we know from its *in situ* farm shop in Snowdonia. T and I were also given what was described as 'the best chocolate brownie in the known universe': apparently William Shatner had told the bakers that this was the case, so it must be true. Who could argue with Capt Kirk? But they were excellent. We had a pleasant lunch in the Southwark Tavern – I gather that the Globe, which was not serving food, will allow you to bring in snacks from the market, which is pretty civilised.

In addition to this primarily gastronomic experience, I also fitted in a visit to the Wellcome Collection: a very interesting display of charms collected by folklorist Edward Lovett, and with accompanying artworks by Felicity Powell, made of wax carved onto the backs of mirrors. Lots of acorn charms, to ward off lightning: obviously a besetting Victorian fear. Some of the collection is in the Cuming Museum and the Pitt Rivers. And the Wellcome also had a display of Mexican exvoto paintings on tin roofing tiles, thanking the saints for rescue and aid. Some gruesome pictures of people being mown down by electric trams, setting themselves on fire, and falling off telegraph poles. The saints must be busy.

The Town Ritual
This has been a tough winter for Glastonbury, what with the snow and the economy, so when a fellow shopkeeper suggested jokingly on Facebook that we do a morale-boosting town-wide ritual, for the prosperity and health of the community, a lot of people thought this might be a nice idea. We ended up with about thirty – thirty five people.

Jamie and I led the ritual: we lit a censer at the Market Cross and everyone wrote their wishes on paper and cast them into the fire. Then, with the fire still smouldering, we walked up the High St to the candlelit White Spring – an amazing space now, loud with water cascading down through the inside of the hill. Jamie did a ritual to Morgan Le Fay, and the group made a libation of milk, then some people stayed inside the spring and the rest of us walked up the Tor. It was intensely cold, with a completely clear sky and the huge full moon hanging over the tower, Orion striding away to the south with Sirius bright at his heels. I did a ritual to Gwyn (who is linked with Orion as the Hunter), and the group made an offering of honey (I hope no one subsequently treads in this and skids off the edge of the hill). Then we walked down again with all the fields sparkling in the moonlight beyond.

What it Says on the Tin
I have a new job at the local college. One of my new teaching colleagues lives in Glastonbury, so I have done what I did at the university and come out of the broom closet as quickly as possible, in as natural a conversational circumstance as possible. In this region, it's fairly easy: 'My partner runs shops in

Glastonbury." "Oh, what do you sell?" "Oh, you know, typical Glastonbury – clothes, jewellery, that sort of thing. We're called Witchcraft Ltd – more or less what it says on the tin."

At this point, my interlocutor typically reacts by being faintly amused, faintly interested, and usually asks a few questions which, in general, are well informed ('are you a witch or a Wiccan,' for instance). Yesterday, my colleague asked me what I thought of the witchcraft museum in Boscastle, as she'd done some historical research down there.

If I'm speaking to one of the more conservative rural types, I usually just leave it as 'typical Glastonbury', which everyone understands around here. There might be a few mother-in-law-on-her-broomstick jokes, but that's about it.

Turn to Jesus. Or the Buddha.

We keep getting notes about turning to Jesus or the Buddha written on the back of cornflake packets and shoved under the door of the shop. I know who is doing this, and she is a poor, troubled soul, largely harmless. She also left a tiny china Welsh dresser on the step.

The madwoman who ranted at the boys for practising black magic some while ago came in and apologised, which surprised us all. This came about because a mutual friend, who is undergoing domestic violence, lost her temper with Madwoman ("You're always saying you're so spiritual but when I was walking around with a black eye last week, those boys are the only ones who offered to do a damn thing! This town is full of people on an ego trip and you're one of them; no one cares except the people who you say are summoning demons" etc etc. This seems to have struck home).

What's That?

Last week, Jamie was approached by a teacher at a local school to ask if she could bring her early teen class into Witchcraft to learn a bit about real witches (they're studying Macbeth). They did this,

Jamie did some palm reading, and has just had a dozen thank you' letters, which are priceless.

"It was really weird but in a good way!"

"I am still getting over the fact that I will marry a rich husband and wondering if I should give up school now?"

"I didn't believe in real witches or wizards until you read Harry's mind and told him what vegetable he was thinking of!" (Jamie said: 'crappy mind reading trick always works.')

Jamie himself being only twenty-four (in my head, he's about forty five), did not patronise the kids. With a probably illegal disregard for health, safety or appropriacy, we left the shop as it was, causing a number of 'what's THAT?' questions:

"What's THAT?" [pointing at large wooden penis]

Jamie: "It's a large wooden cock."

[Teacher spits coffee across room.]

They were, however, much more interested in the coyote's foot.

Anyway, the teacher has asked if she can bring them next year and it is generally held to have been a great success.

Post-Modernism

Me [on Facebook, to a friend]: Your children have just been into the shop insisting that they require Curse Breaking Incense, as an ogre has turned their hair yellow.

Alas, I have been unable to help as I don't think even our incense is up to the job of dealing with ogres.

My friend: Aha, this may be the drawback in validating multiple realities and discourses with one's children. No doubt shortly I'll have to manifest crumpets out of thin air. Oh how I wish I was Mrs Weasley.

Monday Nights

White stuff started falling from the sky again yesterday. Not much, but it's very cold, and we have no central heating (although we do have one open fire), because I am waiting for the oil company to deliver. I am contemplating the adoption of a 'house hat.'

We spent all yesterday in town – we have decided to run a series of Monday talks, on basic magical practice, due mainly to the number of people coming out of local covens etc saying that they haven't learned anything. We seem to be sweeping up the disgruntled at the moment – I had someone else at a workshop who has bailed out of another form of training as none of her (perfectly valid) questions were answered and she was told to 'just trust.' This is a variant of the old teacher's standby 'We'll do that next week,' i.e. 'I have no idea.' It's either laziness, ignorance, or power tripping. When science – which has much more tangible results than magic – has students in the lab pretty much from the get-go, I fail to see why High Priestesses etc would try to repress progress unless it's due to personal power grabbing.

Although I have found that the more knowledgeable someone is – Ronald Hutton, Janet Farrar – the more willing they are to share that knowledge and the more anxious they are that people actually learn. Funny, that.

*

Meanwhile the local free listings paper is advertising a water ceremony, followed by a workshop on how to improve your spiritual connection with nature. It's billed as being outside… if it doesn't rain.

*

Since Jamie and I did our pro-prosperity and anti-negativity ritual in town, Glastonbury seems to have been turned on its head. Our own stability seems to have greatly increased in a number of areas. There are some significant changes happening around us – most seem really positive, although there was a major episode elsewhere in the town (more about this in due course) which has today manifested in threatening behaviour affecting about a dozen people, aggravated assault, the summoning of an extremely tall new policeman whom everyone now fancies, and the proposed tasering of a suspect. And that's just the business community.

*

Woman in shop, staring intently at Jamie: This is *lovely* music. I think it must have a real *connection* to you. It brings back *memories* for you, doesn't it?

Jamie: [thinks: WTF?] Yes. Sarah Brightman is my godmother.

Woman: I knew it! She's spiritual, isn't she?

Jamie: Actually, she's a demonologist.

Woman: A...?

Jamie: Yes, she's been a devotee of Astaroth for years.

Woman: Who...?

Jamie: Dressed in scarlet, a consort of Lucifer... Sarah's down with all that. Why do you think she's had such a long singing career?

Woman: Well, I never knew that.

Jamie: No, she keeps pretty quiet about it. But you know, she's got the big hair, the scarlet dresses... bit of a giveaway.

On the Other Side...

I read the tarot, and am good at it, but although I get what I would term precognitive flashes very occasionally with regard to myself, I am not psychic.

Glastonbury has a lot of 'psychics'. My friend went to someone, accompanied by another woman whom she introduced only by name. The psychic started getting messages from my friend's mother, passing on information from the spirit world, and giving my friend advice about her health.

My friend let this run for a bit before turning to the woman at her side and saying 'So, Mum, what do *you* think about all this?'

A tip: if you're not psychic enough to tell whether someone's mum is dead or alive, let alone actually in the room... you're probably not very psychic at all.

Snowdrops

Today has seen a trip to the South Coast, heading down through Dorset and some extremely pretty villages: snowdrops are out like a white carpet in many places amongst the little thatched cottages, and we stopped to walk the dogs on the edge of a woodland verge which was covered in them, underneath the hazel catkins. Daffodils are late this year, due to the snow, I assume. But it is definitely all moving on towards spring.

It's For...

Trevor: [in moment of male entitlement] Where are all my socks? And my shirts???

Me: Have you looked in the airing cupboard?

Trevor: The what?

Me: It's a cupboard with a hot water tank in it. You know, the one that's been in the back bedroom for the twenty-five years you've lived in this house?

Trevor: I thought that was for drying cats.

Overheard

Trevor, in kitchen talking to the cat: "Your latest fictional creation, the vignette entitled "Sidney Has Not Had His Breakfast", needs a certain amount of work..."

*

It will soon be International Talk Like a Pirate Day, and we do like to celebrate it, but in absence of a stuffed Parrot, I have the next best thing. Lily pup has clambered over me, the Racing Post, and the back of the armchair, and is currently sitting on my shoulder. All fifty plus pounds of her. I WISH I had my camera...

They're in a Meeting

Jamie: [over the phone] Hello, Witchcraft Limited?

Woman: I want to talk to the dead!

Jamie: I'm afraid they're not here right now. [*refrains from adding: they're in a meeting*]

Woman: No! I mean – I want to talk to dead people!

Jamie: Okaaaaay, have you tried – Ouija board/visiting reputable spiritualist/actual necromancy?

Woman: No, and I don't want to spend any money.

*

Female Customer [who has had run-in with J at a psychic fair]: *walks into shop*: What are *you* doing here?

Jamie: I work here.

Female Customer: But there's usually a gentleman here.

Jamie: Yes, that's my boss.

Female Customer: And why has he employed *you*?

Jamie: Because I'm phenomenally good at my job.

Female Customer: [wisely decides to change subject; looks at four foot statue of King Tut, which, okay, is in the somewhat-ghastly-but-they-sell category] You've changed it since last month!

Jamie: It's the same one that was here last month.

Female Customer: It used to be bigger.

Jamie: Perhaps you've shrunk. That happens when you get old.

Customer, amazingly, not only bought the statue, but thanked Jamie for carrying it to her car. Maybe we should abuse them more.

Birthday

I was teaching but we went out to dinner in the evening, at the Manor House Inn at Ditcheat, which I highly recommend. Trevor had lemon sole and the cheese board, and I had rabbit and turnip casserole, which was much nicer than it sounds, and a passion-fruit crème brûlée.

Then we got outside and found that the car battery had gone flat, so we went back into the pub and threw ourselves on its collective mercy. A very kind couple interrupted their evening and went to fetch jump leads. While we were waiting an old gent came up and said that he had lived in Ditcheat for 83 years and everyone was kind to each other: this would appear to be true.

My Uncle

I called Dad earlier this evening and apparently his brother Eric died last night, narrowly missing my birthday (for which I am, selfishly, grateful). He was 92, going on 93, and probably died of pneumonia: they will be holding a post mortem, which has annoyed the entire family as no one sees the point. So we don't know when the funeral will be.

My Aunt Edna died some years ago, after a long struggle with her health. They'd been married for decades and been through a lot. Eric was a chemist and ran a small pharmacy in Swansea, having put himself through university after he came out of the army after the war. He retired not long after the pharmacy was raided, and he and my aunt were tied to chairs overnight, by a couple of heroin addicts who later turned out to be theology students from Lampeter Uni: obviously not having taken much of the theology to heart.

My Aunt

Dammit, now my *aunt* has died, a week after her brother. Dilys was ninety four. Dad is the last of those five siblings, now.

I don't know what she died of, but I just spoke to my cousin's husband and he says she went downhill over the last couple of weeks – Eric's death presumably has not helped but Dilys wasn't really that compos mentis and it's hard to know whether she would have taken it in. Anyway, she was in reasonable health up until a fortnight ago, and she died this afternoon (at home with her daughter by her side).

The family is reeling somewhat, as can be supposed. We're not going to make Eric's funeral on Tuesday as my cousin wants something quiet, but I will be heading down to Pembrokeshire for Dilys'.

Be Playful...

Came into Witchcraft Ltd this morning to find that Phineas the strange small cat has gleefully knocked all the business cards off the counter and spread them over the floor, in the manner of strange small cats first thing in the morning.

There is also a little bowl of 'goddess messages' on the counter (small slips of card with the name of a goddess and a one-line message for your day).

Phineas had not knocked the bowl over, but one of the cards was on the floor. When I picked it up, it read 'BAST: remember to be playful.'

*

To the thief who stole a large crystal tipped wand missing from the shop today – it is a VERY, VERY bad mistake to steal from a witch...

She's the One....

We had to collect a car from the garage this morning so I ended up going into college very early, about 7.45. The refectory was shut, but staff were around, and I turned the corner to hear a woman say, "Yes, she's the one who had to wash all the penises."

Then she realised a stranger was present and clapped her hand over her mouth. At the 'WTF?' look on my face she explained that they were props used for one of the sex education classes...

Come the Glorious Revolution

It has come to my attention that 'spelling is for the middle classes'.

This is from the occultist who punched a fellow speaker at the Occult Conference. Also a person who got busted for writing positive reviews of his own work on Amazon. Presumably fair competition in the literary marketplace is a filthy capitalist habit upheld only by the smug bourgeoisie.

Ouija

We are still doing a series of 'back to basics' on Monday nights and tonight was the turn of the Ouija board, which we did upstairs in the pub, plus séance.

There is an issue with the spirit world, in that people long deceased may not have been literate:

Séance members: What is your name?

Entity: Mjjkuthm!

Séance members: Okay, do you actually know how to spell?

Entity: [pause, glass slowly moves] No...

Funeral

I drove down to Pembrokeshire on Tuesday morning – it's about three and a half hours from here. Arrived in good time and caught up with my family – two of my cousins had flown in from Mombasa at 5 a.m. but still made the funeral in time. No one was late and it all went smoothly. The local canon, who knew my aunt for twenty-two years, gave the address: it was a very standard Church of Wales service and appropriate for my aunt. The flowers were glorious. Then we walked behind the coffin to the cemetery and buried her, before going back to the house for a vast quantity of sandwiches, tea and cake (I told you it was Welsh).

In the hearse, returning, my cousin's girlfriend apparently said, in a clear and carrying voice (please insert S Welsh accent in which every syllable is enunciated and some extra ones put in): "So, is that the vicar whose wife is a prost-stit-tute, then?"

I have no idea where this came from as Canon G appears wholly blameless of this kind of thing. My cousin P said that the hearse noticeably speeded up as the undertaker switched into manual and slammed his foot on the accelerator, as in 'get this woman out of the car before she says anything else.'

At the house, the local vicar – a man like a dishevelled bloodhound – was obviously impressed by the Canon's appearance. "Isn't he tidy?" he kept saying. "Isn't he neat?" He also remarked to my cousin that it was a nice deep grave, 'not like at the local church.' I had a brief chat to him. "St Paul says we should weep with those who weep and laugh with those who laugh," he said, "But I seem to keep making everyone laugh."

Due to the closure of part of the eastbound M4, most of my relatives then left, leaving Dilys' immediate family and me, so we broke out the wine, cooked a lasagne and ate more cake. At 10, three of us went out into the dark and fed the molly lambs (the ones who won't drink from their mum – I'm assuming this comes from 'molly coddle.') It was nice, after a day of speaking to people, to sit in the quiet barn with a bottle and the squeaking lambs.

South Wales

I came back yesterday via St David's Cathedral – a lovely place in early spring, even on a cold day. The daffodils were out around the cathedral and there were jackdaws tumbling and fighting in the wind. I had lunch in Solva – a nice new cafe called Thirty Five, on the waterfront – and then drove slowly back along the dramatic coast road which winds around St Bride's Bay.

Since I had the whole day, I did not take the motorway on the way back but the old A40 through Llandeilo, Llandovery and Brecon, where I stopped at the foot of the castle and bought some lamb chops with only slight guilt. Beautiful countryside at this time of year, with banks of crocuses and snowdrops. At home, all our primroses are out, with some miniature daffs, and Trevor has been hacking all the ivy away from the front wall.

London

I have spent the last weekend in London, running a writing workshop – a big thank you to all those who attended and particularly to Farah and Edward, as this would not have happened without them.

E very kindly took me to the local noodle bar (a great place) on Friday night, which was enlivened by the appearance of the fire brigade and the apparent collapse of a neighbouring building, but the tape that they placed around it was gone on Saturday so one assumes they fixed whatever the problem was. We also went to the local Turkish cafe, which is also a cultural centre, on several occasions, resulting in an enormous amount of leftovers.

On Saturday night I made it up to Walthamstow to go to the pub with my friend Elle, which was very pleasant, and yesterday pottered about London. I walked down the King's Road, discovering a new tea atelier (that's what they call themselves) run by a gay American couple who are clearly very enthusiastic about tea. They gave me some free Earl Grey. After lunch at Benihana, I walked along the Embankment to the Tate and had a look at the Turner collection (also a large knitted pyramid thing. I think Turner has the edge, put it that way). Then went up to Covent Garden and touched down at Treadwells who very kindly made me tea and sent me round the corner to a South Indian restaurant before a book launch: this was to celebrate Philip Carr-Gomm's book on poet, artist and druid Ross Nichols, whom P knew well. Regrettably I had little time at the launch due to an early train, but

I did speak to a few people, mainly P's co-author on the *Book of English Magic*, Richard Heygate (who as well as being a SF fan is also a baronet, I now realise). Needless to say, I also picked up some books, including a 1923 copy of the Occult Review as a present for Trevor.

Actually Beyond Words

Have just got in to find that Lily has deconstructed a £120 tweed jacket.

I think it is recoverable as she has ripped it down the hems of one sleeve, but eaten the buttons.

When...

...everyone you meet is a special snowflake. Just why do so many of them think that entitles them to some sort of control over your thinking...?

Zodiac and Garden

On Thursday last week, Trevor and I went to interview John Wadsworth, who is running a course in Glastonbury based on Katharine Maltwood's Glastonbury Zodiac. They take one symbol a month, do walks in the relevant bit of the countryside, and focus on the symbolism of each zodiac sign. This sounds simple, but it's actually quite a sophisticated course, from what John was saying (he was citing Frances Yates' memory theatres, for instance).

Since John is currently staying in the Chalice Well retreat house, it seemed an ideal opportunity to walk round the well gardens, and so we did: they were beautiful at this time of year, with daffodils and hellebore fringing the paths. The gardens always seem to be full of robins. I bought the new history of the gardens, which has just come out in paperback – well worth a look.

Pagan Federation Conference

Pagan Federation conference yesterday – we attended two of the talks (Jules Vayne on chaos magick and Chris Crowley on grail legends in Brittany). The Folk Theatre once more failed to show up – they've done this before – leaving a two hour hole in the middle of the afternoon schedule. No comment, except praise for the people who stepped into the breach.

We also met a most interesting man named Simon Costin, who is trying to set up a Museum of British Folklore. He's just been involved in a Vogue shoot, as apparently their July issue is on the theme of folklore, and model Erin O'Connor has been involved in the museum's launch. I think this is a great project, and the more publicity that Simon gets, the better.

Defence Against the Dark Arts

I have been working today. Jamie has been running a Defence Against the Dark Arts workshop and hopefully will be around to run it again, unlike his predecessors at Hogwarts. Thus my afternoon schedule has gone something like: *get cup of tea/enter takings into spreadsheet/launch malevolent psychic attach against students/clean under counter.* It's a great job if you don't weaken.

Bang!

In other news, Trevor appears to have inadvertently thrown his mobile phone into the heart of a bonfire:

Me: Are you sure you didn't leave it in the shop?

Bonfire: BANG!

Trevor: Fairly sure.

A Man at the Door

I'm aware that some of these entries may sound pretty weird. I am reporting things as they happened, and one is obviously free to put one's own interpretation on them.

Jamie's friend P is down from Manchester at the moment, and the two of them ran a voodoo service last night. Having been to the one back in the autumn, I had some idea what to expect, although P is not a priest, and comes from a different tradition (he's also an Italian Catholic). This service was a lot smaller – only four of us. It went well, with quite a lot of possession (not myself, although I did get a rather odd sense of being mentally displaced for a moment, as though someone had taken hold of my brain and was attempting to remove it), and it was very low key – any ideas of people throwing themselves about and entering hysterical states are not accurate.

I spent half an hour or so upstairs, as one of the spirits objected, though politely, to my clothes (which were black – you're supposed to wear white).

Towards the end the inevitable person banged on the door. This always happens during rituals and unless we are outside and have to engage, the best thing to do is carry on and ignore them. I looked round and saw a man looking in through the thin net curtain that covers the door. When that's up, we can see out but people can't really see in, so I ignored Demanding Man and carried on. Jamie has had visits from some of the local street people asking for this and that. This one had long hair and an unpleasant, aggressive expression – it was a very odd face, but some people round here do look fairly odd. I could not tell what his skin colour was, because of the curtain. When I looked round again, he had gone and then a particularly difficult spirit showed up (via P), asking for a knife, which Jamie refused to give him, and he left.

So that was that and we finished the service. When we were having a quick discussion, I mentioned the man at the door and asked Jamie if he thought it was the same person who had been banging on the door a few days ago. Blank looks from everyone else. What man at the door? they asked. He knocked, I said – quite hard. In fact, he hammered. We summoned Jack, from upstairs. If someone knocks, you hear it throughout the building – it's an old, rattly door and shakes the building. Nope, said Jack, looking blank, didn't hear a thing, and he had been sitting directly above the doorway.

So, oh. The difficult spirit is one Baron Criminel, whose name is a bit of a giveaway – he is a sort of spirit of murder, among other things. Whoever he was, I am glad I didn't answer the door.

Quoth the Raven...

...what the raven actually quoth was 'Ek!Ek!Ek!' followed by a duck and shuffle of the neck and a quick grab at the fingers of the person who was unwise enough to try to tickle him.

He appeared in Benedict St this afternoon. His name is Bran and he comes from the local falconry: his keeper has been showing him around town as a publicity exercise. We might be hiring him for a ritual at some point. He is a wily, clever bird, like most ravens, and capable of working out the combination lock to his aviary.

The last time I saw one so close was on Skomer Island – amongst the wild flock of some thirty birds was a raven named Friendly, so called because he used to march up to tourists and wish them good morning. He'd obviously been tamed and released to join his wild relatives.

26,000 Years Ago

I also made it up to the druidic meeting in Bristol, where we did some work with arrowheads – 10,000 years old, from a private collection. Remarkable, to handle something that old. I have friends down on the Gower who regularly visit Pavilland Cave, home of the Red Lady burial – the 'lady' was actually a twenty-one year old man, living 26,000 years ago (possibly more). I find that my imagination gives out when it comes to that kind of time span.

Speak! Oh Wait, You Already Have

Just had another complaint from a customer about one of the local psychics, for passing on messages from people who aren't, um, actually dead. This has happened before...in one case, the message was from someone on the other side...of the psychic's front door. The psychic in question is allegedly going to set up a spiritualist church. The mind boggles.

There is a place for the false medium's act, is all I'm saying.

The Write Fantastic

We made it up to Oxford yesterday to the celebrations of the Write Fantastic, a writers' collective which I have recently joined – good company, Many thanks to Juliet and the team for organising such a good event. It was held at St Hilda's College – a lovely venue for this sort of thing (though it did lack coffee. Author Geoff Ryman is now the new God of Coffee, you'll be pleased to hear. I'm sure he'll do a great job).

I did not attend any of the panels apart from the one I was on, which did rather resemble a bar conversation without any alcohol. A riveted audience now know why I don't own an Aga, and why it's not a good idea to travel across the Sargasso Sea in the company of a woman in a gold bikini (thank you Ian Watson).

Trevor and I spent some of the afternoon wandering around Oxford and got sucked into an exhibition on eccentricity, as you do. This was mainly devoted to Oxford's scientific luminaries and featured one Ellen Willmott, who as well as devising a turning device for wooden implements practised a form of guerilla gardening in her declining years and used to seed friends' flower beds with giant thistles.

We had lunch in the Cape of Good Hope, and subsequently dinner in the Quod – all very pleasant. We made it back to Somerset in two and a half hours and were in bed by 10 pm, which if you've been dining in Oxford is not bad going.

*

I did not have to take the coffee shop at their word regarding the temperature of their wares, after I poured half of a large takeaway mug down my front while trying to re-open the shop door – chic...

*

Jamie has got me a packet of new incense sticks.

It is a blend called: 'Queen of Fucking Everything.'

March

Raven and Wine

Trevor and I went up to Bath on Monday, to a small trade show (some beautiful jewellery made out of rough-cut aquamarines, garnets, amber etc), and thence to lunch at our usual tapas place and a pint at the Raven. I have now managed to locate the Raven, which I usually lose, and the cheese shop: both are in Quiet Street.

We also went to a wine tasting at the Bishop's Palace in Wells last night – a very good selection, including a Beaujolais producer and one of the New Zealand wineries. I am not a big fan of Beaujolais, finding it too light, but the same producers did have a very nice Pouilly-Fuisse and there was some good Syrah elsewhere from one of the other producers. My tasting notes, which are not the height of subtlety, include 'meh', 'bleah,' 'wow!' and 'Trevor thinks...' as Trevor's palate is a lot more reliable than mine, but, like amateur art critics, I know what I like and since the whole point of it on a personal level is subjectivity...

Changes

We are saying goodbye to our longest serving employee in a few minutes. I have bought her a big bunch of flowers and we are taking her to the pub. She's been with Witchcraft Ltd since before I came on the scene – about nine years in all, and she's leaving because she was diagnosed with breast cancer two weeks ago. It's in its very early stages and her prognosis is very good, but, even so, we are very sad to see J leaving under these circumstances. I suspect that when she has left, we'll realise just how much she had done to keep this business going and I plan to tell her so.

Feeding the Lions

Cat is shrieking outside kitchen door (starving, on verge of death etc).

Take out handful of dried cat biscuits.

Head towards bowl, which is on the top of the freezer out of the way of the dogs.

Sister of cat (Pickle) panics, steps in bowl, catapults bowl and remaining large portion of cat food over floor, narrowly missing my head.

Dog cleans up.

Cat is now very disgruntled because starving, on verge of death etc. Sigh.

*

Could really use a full day in the office to get orders out now, but STILL waiting for the car to be picked up for repairs. Stuck at home with Rottweiler girls beating each other up. And can't do my essay because my laptop is – in the office of course – and the power lead is locked inside the boot of the car – sigh...

The Thelekite

Jamie: Can I help you?

Black Clad Customer: [looking scornfully at books] I DOUBT you would have anything that would interest ME.

Jamie: I see. And why would that be?

Black Clad Customer: Because I am a THELEKITE – a follower of Aleister Crowley!

Jamie: So... do your rituals only work on windy days?

Black Clad Customer: ...sorry?

Jamie: It's "Thelemite..."

Cue swift exit of customer.

Banned

A while back, I banned an acquaintance from my premises – she had what might best be described as a mental health episode in

Glastonbury (this consisted of exposing herself to my staff and customers, shouting and cursing, and – as far as we can determine – posting shit through the door of the pub that asked her not to smoke on their premises). She's now been sectioned and has written a reproachful letter to me, which does contain an apology (accepted) but which might also be construed as something of an attempted guilt trip. I do, in fact, realise that she has been ill and isn't entirely responsible for her actions.

But what age has brought is, unfortunately, the realisation that I can't bring myself to care. I have a partner who has been seriously ill, I have very elderly parents and relatives who are currently seriously ill and who need my support, and life over the past decade has been extremely difficult in a number of respects. I have got to the point where I no longer care if I'm seen as the bad guy: if that gets people off my back, then well and good, and if that means I am seen to treat people unfairly, then tough.

For some years now, both Trevor and I have been casting people off the communal sled and I can't bring myself to regret this, because it means that we have ourselves survived emotionally, and have been able to support the people who are closest, and who need that support. I can only conclude that part of becoming middle aged has, for me, been an embracing of the inner bitch: it's perhaps not a good thing to note that one grows worse as one grows older, but it does seem to be the way of things. I know a number of people who have cast the toxic out of their lives, whether friends or family, and will defend their need to do that, at least, if not their right.

*

A friend came into the shop today with his small son:

Son [looking at incense labels]: Dad, what does lust mean?

Friend [without discernible pause] It's when you can't find something.

Son [losing interest]: Oh.

*

Cobweb (our elderly cat): I want to sit by you.
Me: You can't. I'm having my dinner.
Cat: But I want to sit by you.
Me: I repeat. You can't. I'm having my dinner.
Cat: I'm GOING to sit by you.
Cat leaps.
Cat lands in middle of dinner.
Me: What the HELL!?
Cat: Wheeeee!
Leaps out of plate, kicking dinner across the settee.
Cat: now I am sitting by you. Ooooh! Crème fraiche.

*

Yesterday saw the cursing of a local businessman plastered all over the press – someone sent him a curse, although a very badly done one, in a sympathy card and it has hit the press.

Vernal Equinox
The week has been greatly enlivened by the presence of writer Kari Sperring, who very kindly put up with being terrorized by dogs (dragged into swamp, sat on, bounced at), cats (woken up, 'offering' left on bedroom floor in middle of night), this house (sudden failure of internet, insufficient breakfast materials) and Glastonbury itself (enough said). However, we did manage to visit Wells market, have several civilised meals, see the glorious Chalice Well – particularly lovely right now – and invent a new game: Knife/Dog/Trousers, which is rather like Paper/Scissors /Stone and is based on Welsh compensatory law. Also in the works: 'Lesbian Trapeze Artists of Avalon,' a new novel which will deal with Pythagoras' renegade daughter. You might have to wait a while for it, though.

*

The thunderstorm that has been promising to appear for the last couple of weeks has finally done so, improving the local mood no end in spite of torrents of monsoon-like rain. I've been in the shop, working on various manuscripts (my own and other people's) and aiming for a quiet evening tonight: we have a joint of lamb and it's starting to look like an evening for a roast... I have been spending most evenings this week in an outrageous and decadent manner: catching up with the boxed set of *Coast*. Although we did go to the pub last night.

*

I have been reading Jack Parson's *Freedom is a Two Edged Sword* – known as the 'James Dean of the occult,' Parsons was a remarkably character – a follower of Crowley and ceremonial magician who was also a rocket scientist at Pasadena. He died in 1952, having blown himself up. I'm not wild about the libertarian cast of his political essays, but he was an interesting individual.

*

Cue conversation in the pub:

T: We'll have to write it into the interview procedure in future. "Have you ever been sectioned?"

Me: I don't think that's legal.

Jamie: The interview notes are already a yard thick! "Have you ever been abducted by aliens?" "Have you ever thought of yourself as the Queen of the Fairies?" Just say to them: "Do you have the Crazy? If so, what sort? Is it the Sad? The Really *Really* Sad? Is it the 'lots of people in my head'?"

G (who runs psychic fairs]: I employed X on the door, but she was mad. Now I've got D on the door. He's mad too, but in a different way.

Jamie, to G: But you do know some *spectacular* knobheads.

And This is Where Going Outside Gets You...

Henry has not appeared all day: did not come in for breakfast etc. Looked on the roadsides etc, went down the field. Eventually went out the back, where I have been in and out all day, calling, and heard sad howls coming from the middle of the bramble thicket. By now it was 6 pm and the light was going fast. Could not find secateurs. Beat back brambles with hands and crawled, on my stomach, into the thicket, which is about 6-10 feet across. Afraid that he was injured, I managed to locate H, who got up and walked off. Cursing mightily, went back in house to fetch cat food tin, came back outside, Sid materialised out of dusk and went to fetch H, who trotted out of the thicket and demanded his tea. Now look as though I have been dragged through a hedge backwards, which is not surprising as this is exactly what has just happened. I have found brambles in my underwear. Was not going to pour a glass of wine this evening. Change of plan.

*

Jamie looked out of the window of the shop and saw five teenagers (four boys and a girl) storm a moving car in the street. The driver, naturally irate, got out and decked two of them – he must have been an amateur boxer, because he felled both of them with a punch apiece, which is quite hard to do. He was then attacked by the girl, shrieking and punching, and (being either gallant or sexist, depending on your point of view) said, 'Look, love, I'll give you three chances and then you're on your own.' She did not listen, and continued to attack him, so he punched her in the face and knocked her out as well – by this time Jamie, who was phoning the police, said the road was littered with unconscious bodies like something out of the Keystone Cops. Then the remaining two tried to drag the driver's friend out of the car as well, and the friend laid both of them out.

*

Yesterday was brightened by the appearance of a skunk – on a lead held by a woman who runs a ferret sanctuary. She let me hold the skunk, who promptly fell asleep with his feet curled around my necklace. In disentangling him, a ring worn by his owner got tangled up with one of mine, creating a knot of women and skunk in the middle of the shop.

Teaching Science Fiction

I got up to town by lunchtime on Friday and was met by S, who took me over to Cthulhu Towers and subsequently to a very nice pub on Broadway Market, the Dove, where we had lunch. I spent the afternoon in Forbidden Planet, doing a drive-by signing, and in Covent Garden, then returned to the Dove for dinner (where I managed not to get embroiled in a row that a couple on the next table were having: the sort where they keep turning to you and apologising aggressively in the hope that you'll express an opinion, whereupon they will round on you).

Saturday morning, I made my way up to Hendon, met the class, and went for lunch at a local noodle bar, which was to become our default cafe. We did three books in my section of the weekend – *Heritage of Hastur, Golden Witchbreed,* and my own *Winterstrike*, with a loose theme of women and science fantasy.

In the evening, we managed to avoid the football and found a nice Sri Lankan restaurant in Hendon.

On Sunday, writer and critic Roz Kaveney and I went back up to Hendon and taught, and since my session was in the morning this time I went down to Hampstead for a walk on the Heath and tea in Carluccio's: I haven't been to Hampstead for some considerable time, but used to go regularly in the early 90s as we had friends in the area. It doesn't seem to have changed much, although I'm sure its residents would disagree.

*

Getting depressed working on a very quiet day in The Magick Box, and in comes Rae Beth – author of several excellent books – including what is still one of the best introductions to the Craft – Hedgewitch. Of course we conversed on such pagan topics as the economy, the Great Depression, and how history is written and written about – sometimes I remember I love my job.

The English Riviera
...we have been to it. We went down to Paignton on Tuesday night to attend an esoteric publishing event, organised by astrologer Sasha Fenton and held in Paignton's quite ludicrously elaborate Town Hall. The event was fun – there were some good talks and I learned something, namely how to read fortunes with playing cards, rather than the Tarot per se. We had dinner at an Italian restaurant in Torquay, and stayed over at a very nice B&B – nothing like Fawlty Towers – driving back first thing yesterday morning.

Me and My Yoni
An upcoming event in Glastonbury is advertising a 'Yoni massage workshop,' an event which has caused much hilarity among the town's female population (God only knows what the men are saying. Apart from making plans to hire a ladder and a pair of binoculars. Or, uh, not).

I came across a description of this today and it has reinforced my heartfelt wish not to explore my sexuality with anyone other than Mr Jones or a qualified GP:

These precious jewels were then included into my life in a way that I deeply felt more in tune with my body and sexuality. I became sensitively aware of my Yoni's 'voice'.

Wonder what it said?

Words Fail Me...

...with regard to the woman who approached Trevor in the street and asked if we'd be willing to breed our Rottweiler with her Rottweiler.

Not without a sudden leap of technology, given that both dogs are bitches.

This is why some people shouldn't be allowed to keep dogs.

I Am of the Cat Nation

A woman went into the Benedict St shop last week and made overtures to Phineas, J and J's strange small cat. Phineas bolted under a table, as usual, and the woman announced that she 'was of the cat nation,' whatever *that* means, and had an 'affinity' with nature's felines. Phineas did eventually come out again, and to everyone's secret delight, bit her.

Visitors

Given the nature of Somerset, I rarely find myself drinking with Hasidic Jews, but such was not the case tonight: we went to one of the village pubs, the rather lovely Ashcott Inn, for a late dinner after a business meeting, and met a group of young men from London who are here on a retreat. They'd spent the previous night in the Ashcott and have left their mark on a photograph of cricketer W G Grace, who did indeed sport a magnificent beard: his image now also has a little pair of paper ringlets and a biro'd yarmulke.

They're about twenty, and English is not their first language. One of them is an SF fan, however, so that was that. If you're reading this, I hope you enjoy the book!

However, we were not at all whelmed by the Pike and Musket down the road, who wouldn't let these guys in. Anyone who doubts that anti-Semitism is alive and well in this country need probably look no further, and neither Trevor nor I will be drinking there in future*. But kudos to people from what I understand to be a strict sect, who on coming to a sometimes notoriously insular part of the country almost immediately went out and talked to the locals.

In fact, I cursed the P&M and it closed down shortly afterwards.

*

[In the street in Glastonbury]
Woman [addressing my friend C]: Are you Boudicca?
C: Er, no.
Woman [darkly]: She wants my knickers.
C:…?
Woman: Where's the doctor's surgery?

C told her. Probably just as well.

*

We have a rumour mill in the shop – Jamie made it out of cardboard in a Blue Peter moment.

This one isn't the latest rumour, but it's only just reached me and it's a classic. It probably comes from Rat Girl.

Apparently, I am 'being abused' – not physically, but psychologically and probably magically.

Because, as one of the main feminist SF writers in this country, I have no mind of my own, I am so firmly under Trevor's thumb that I simply do his bidding.

If you know me, you know how impressionable and easily led I am.

An adjoining, but possibly related, rumour states that Jamie is similarly controlled by me, to the extent that he conducts black magic on other people on my behalf. Because, you know, I'm that powerful. Only, one assumes, not as powerful as Trevor.

If you know Jamie, you know how impressionable and easily led he is.

(There is another rumour which suggests that J controls both T and myself – this stems from a different source, so lacks consistency with (a) and (b).)

*

Middle Aged Woman, floating around the shop: Guess what *I* am???

Jamie: [wearily] What?

MAW: I'm a fairy!

Jamie: Right. Which court?

MAW: What?

Jamie: Seelie or Unseelie?

MAW: [doubtfully] Seelie. I think. [floats some more] Do you know what I need?

Jamie: [actually not meaning to invoke out loud voice] A bath?

MAW: What?

Jamie: Um! Sorry!

MAW: Did you say: a bath?

Jamie: Frankly, yes.

MAW: [inspects underarms, which are not good] Maybe I should.

Revenge of the Night Dog

Me: But you cannot eat your dinner if you won't come down the stairs.

Elder cat: EEEEEEEEEEEEEEEEEEEE!

Me: There are no monsters. Look. Under the chair? Monster free.

Elder cat: There might be a DOOOOOOOOOOOOOOG!

Me: As in, the same dog you slept on the bed with all last night? When you kept purring? And did your laundry?

Elder cat: Those are night dogs. This is different. And... there's that Thing.

Me: Henry. The kitten. Whom you also slept on the bed with.

Whose nose you kiss when you meet him in the kitchen?
Elder cat: That's different.
Me: So are you going to come downstairs?
Elder cat: EEEEEEEEEEEEEEEEEEEEEE!
...and so on...

*

Contemplating a day in the office and wondering whether to take the one-puppy wrecking crew or leave her at home to her diet of potted plants – sigh.

*

Off to a book signing but predictably at closing time – in comes a customer who wants to try an expensive dress on... Let me see – glass of wine, best sale of the day...? Well it IS Rioja – but then SHE is Spanish too – and they don't START shopping until evening…

*

In the unlikely event that our fainting customer of yesterday is reading this: if you claim to have been a '3rd level mage' in your past life but don't know what your 'tradition' is, it is probable that your tradition is Dungeons and Dragons.

*

Jamie to customer, on being asked for a highly poisonous herb by someone who was quite clearly not entirely sane. 'It's my day off'. 'Pardon?'. 'Day off – from idiots' 'Oh – okay' – customer leaves sheepishly... Get your quality Glastonbury insults here! Fresh every day...

*

Only in Glastonbury – 'Hi – I have Cerridwen's cauldron here...'
Which I do.

*

We have news for you. 2012 is already here. A friend has done some proper, non-bullshit research, and the disaster is in 2010. It's a flood.

*

And so the day begins. Lily the puppy killing a ferocious slipper, and me putting a quartz tip on a magic wand. Normal for Glastonbury then!

*

Overheard in a local guest house: "And then I woke up, and saw my feet. And they were a Tibetan demon's feet!"

Epilogue

It's summer again, some months down the line. Henry and Sid are still ruling the household with a paw of iron; Lily and Cass are still falling into ponds and eating things they shouldn't. Of the human *dramatis personae* of Diary Two, Jamie and Jack are running St Martha's Botanica down Benedict Street: call in and see them if you're in town. As I write this epilogue, Jamie is reading Diary Two – his only comment on being told "You're in the book" was – "Can I add stuff?"

Rat Girl lost her business and was obliged to take a job at the local launderette, washing other people's dirty laundry. I'll leave you to decide whether karma works or not.

Exployee has never been seen in Glastonbury again. About a year after I fired her, one of Britain's premier necromancers came back as Jamie and Jack were renovating the shop. "Oh," he said, from the back of the shop, close to where Exployee claimed to have been attacked whilst vacuuming. "Sorry about that. I forgot I'd put that there." And removed a demonic sigil from under a cupboard.

Until the next time...

- END -

Diary of a Witchcraft Shop
By Trevor Jones and Liz Williams

In 2005, fantasy and SF author extraordinaire Liz Williams took the plunge, moving from her beloved Brighton to Glastonbury to live with her partner, Trevor Jones. Trevor ran a witchcraft shop. Liz's life would never be the same again…

"When you find yourself on a London platform shouting into your mobile, 'We haven't got enough demons! Do you want me to order some more?' as folk quietly edge away from you – you know you're running a witchcraft shop."

The original *Diary of a Witchcraft Shop*.
Available now in paperback and eBook from NewCon Press

A Glass of Shadow
Liz Williams
Introduction by Tanith Lee
Cover art by Anne Sudworth

"From the moment you open this collection, you leave the Known behind and enter the brighter, darker, more *actual* possibility that lies just through that door, over that hill…" *Tanith Lee*

"Williams has mastered the art of writing clearly and believably about weird, alien worlds." *The Times*

"Liz Williams' writing awakens the mind and transports the senses. When it has you thus distracted it is also stealthily penetrating the secret heart of things." *Tricia Sullivan.*

"Williams weaves a rich, complicated tapestry that merges life with afterlife, otherworldly with worldly and human with inhuman." *Publishers Weekly*

Liz Williams at her best. Nineteen stories personally selected by the author that delve into our psyche and investigate the fragility of the human condition, that draw aside the veils of mundane reality to reveal hidden truths of this world and beyond. Stories that transports you from the icy Martian wastes of *Winterstrike* to the searing deserts of Kazakhstan, from the exotic streets of Inspector Chen's Singapore Three to the hidden courtyards of Venice. Includes two pieces original to this collection.

Available now from NewCon Press

www.newconpress.co.uk